ON THE CEILING

Au plafond

Éric Chevillard

Le texte de ce roman est traduit et présenté par

JORDAN STUMP

Les presses universitaires du Nebraska, Lincoln et Londres

On the Ceiling

Éric Chevillard

Translated and with an introduction by

JORDAN STUMP

University of Nebraska Press : Lincoln and London

Publication of this book was assisted by a grant
from the National Endowment for the Arts 🌱
© 1997 by Les Éditions de Minuit. Translation and
introduction © 2000 by the University of Nebraska
Press. All rights reserved. ⊗ Manufactured in the
United States of America

Library of Congress Cataloging in Publication Data
Chevillard, Eric.
[Au plafond. English] On the ceiling = Au plafond/
Eric Chevillard; translated and with an introduction
by Jordan Stump.
p. cm. ISBN 0-8032-1504-5 (cloth: alkaline paper) –
ISBN 0-8032-6396-1 (pbk.: alkaline paper) I. Title:
Au plafond. II. Stump, Jordan, 1959– III. Title
PQ2663.H432 A913 2000 843'.914–dc21 00-020179

I can think of no desire quite so widespread in this world as the longing not to live in it – the longing, that is, to live in some other world, one more just, or more interesting, or simply less hostile. Play, religion, reading, drugs: so many forms of human activity, or inactivity, struggle hopefully and tirelessly toward that same elusive goal. But the unfortunate fact of alternative realities is that precisely because they are alternative – which means alternative in relation to something – they have an uncanny tendency to reproduce the failings of our own world. Anyone who has ever spent time on the ceiling is, of course, already quite aware of this.

Like Raymond Roussel or William Burroughs, Éric Chevillard constructs in his novels an instantly recognizable and coherent world to which we might make our escape – a world of curious language and curiouser events, one comfortingly different from our own but also disturbingly familiar: it bristles with challenges to human existence, or at least to human happiness, offering its inhabitants a continuous stream of small irritations and agonizing torments (assuming that there is indeed a difference between the two). For that reason – and, again, as in our own world – the characters of Chevillard's novels have little choice but to dream up the most hopelessly outlandish and breathtakingly brilliant schemes if they are to survive the rigors of their existence. And, as in this life, their projects generally produce not the slightest improvement.

This is the story told again and again in the eight novels Chevillard has published since 1987. He is fascinated by the imperious need we all feel to make life bearable, and by the lengths to which we are willing to go in that pursuit. His characters are prepared to go further than most of us. Not for them, the personal makeover: the tactic they choose is to reshape the world from the ground up. They feel – quite rightly, too – that the fault lies not in themselves but in the universe, and so they set out to right the wrong, one way or another. Furne, the central character of *Le Caoutchouc, décidément* (1992), has ambitious plans for a "radical reform of the system currently in place" that involve, among many other initiatives, shrinking to the size of an eyeball the area of human flesh sensitive to pain, thereby drastically slashing the quantity of discomfort we must endure. On a more modest scale, the unnamed narrator of *Préhistoire* (1994) methodically transforms his lodgings into a simulacrum of an elaborately ornamented paleolithic cave dwelling, rather like the imitation Lascaux visited by tourists today but hermetically sealed off against the world, against every intrusion of modernity, a refuge in which he can live and die undiscovered and undisturbed for tens of thousands of years. Crab, the long-suffering protagonist of *La Nébuleuse du crabe* (1993) – published in translation by the University of Nebraska Press as *The Crab Nebula* (1998) – dreams of rewiring the human respiratory system so that we might cleanse the filthy air around us with our lungs and give breath to undiluted ecstasy. Such projects may well be doomed to failure from the start, but that is not the question here: what matters in Chevillard's novels is less the workability of the solutions his characters propose to life's impossibilities than the elegant reasoning behind their invention and the inelegant logistics of their realization.

On the Ceiling (first published in France in 1997) takes up this same tale once again. But, as always, it does so quite differently from its predecessors: the problems are not the same, nor are the solutions, even if that old impulse to correct a flawed world persists unchanged. This is not an insignificant point; the coexistence of sameness and difference seems to me a fundamental element of Chevillard's writing and of the curious world it creates. For this is a world in which identity and non-identity are forever in doubt: Crab, perhaps his most recognizable character, is so malleable, so open to the influence of those around him, that he is perfectly capable of becoming at the same time an old man and an expectant mother; a bald, redheaded, skinny seven-year-old with jet-black hair; and an athletic, fat old man, and so on – and once he steps into the skin of this Everyman, he finds himself ipso facto entirely unique, monstrous, and alone. Similarly, characters from one book have an unnerving tendency to pop up again in another, in a different shape, to be sure, but nevertheless essentially identical to their forebears: Crab reappears in *On the Ceiling* as Egger, Furne as Kolski, and the title character of *Palafox* (1990) – an odd creature with feathered wings, silky fur, a snout, a tail, a shell, a hand, gills, horns, a stinger, and so forth – pops up in these pages as the loveable Woff (who might well, however, be little more than a humble lapdog).

More unsettlingly still, one novel, *La Nébuleuse du crabe*, reappears under Chevillard's pen as another, *Un Fantôme* (1994): it is the same book, has the same central character, the same loose story, but with a different title and entirely different events. Again and again Chevillard's writing poses a difficult question: Is one thing the same as another or not? Are *La Nébuleuse du crabe* and *Un Fantôme* one book or two? Is Woff Palafox or is he Woff (or is he Crab)? Is the ceiling the opposite of the floor or only another version of the same thing?

Such conundrums lie at the very heart of Chevillard's imagination and of his writing, as will become apparent from the opening lines of *On the Ceiling*. But what will first strike a reader new to Chevillard's work is no doubt his astonishing style: those uncontainable sentences, careening wildly through and over comma splices, mixed metaphors, abrupt anticlimaxes, unruly similes, flashing briefly into three-dimensional existence and then suddenly fading from sight. No matter how it might seem at first glance, Chevillard's writing is always profoundly logical; but the links between ideas often go unstated, or exist only as metaphor, or depend on some ephemeral and impalpable play of language. This is not to say that his writing is obscure, only that it demands the reader's imagination and involvement – and is this not why we read in the first place? Chevillard requires a certain amount of work from the reader, but he pays good wages: having spent some time in the strange world he depicts, we can never again feel quite the same about our own.

I might add that Chevillard also requires a certain amount of work from his translator. It is not only his style and his relentless play with words and images that make him difficult to translate, it is also the extent to which he draws upon a French culture that, although in the end not so different from ours, nevertheless draws on objects and experiences that may not be entirely familiar to American readers. It would be useful for the reader of this book, for instance, to know that trees in French cities are frequently trimmed in such a way as to produce a small number of thick branches protruding from a massive trunk; that an enormous new home for the French national library, the Bibliothèque de France (formerly the Bibliothèque Nationale), has indeed been built in Paris (it opened in 1997); that not so long ago, one did have to pay for the use of portable metal armchairs in Parisian parks (the city used to employ elderly women to circulate through the parks and collect the small fee). But of course much remains the same between our two cultures – the law of gravity, for instance – and, in any case, familiarity and ease of understanding are not really what Chevillard's reader should be after; that would destroy the troublesome magic of his writing. The twists and turns, the reader's sudden swings from incomprehension to revelation and back again, are vital components of the experience of this highly unconventional writer. Those willing to follow that sinuous route will discover one of the most distinctive, funny, and unpredictable voices on the current French literary scene, which, moreover, does not lack for such voices. Like Chevillard, many of these new young writers are being published by Éditions de Minuit: Jean Echenoz, Jean-Philippe Toussaint, Christian Gailly, Marie Ndiaye, Jean-Pierre Chanod, Christian Oster, Eugène Savitzkaya, and many others. This current wealth of eccentric, witty, and deeply intelligent writing does not constitute a school, as we like to think a previous generation of Minuit novelists did (Alain Robbe-Grillet, Nathalie Sarraute, Claude Simon). It does, however, suggest the very healthy state of contemporary writing in France. I find in this situation – and in Chevillard's writing – yet another reason to be grateful to France, and I believe adventurous readers who plunge into *On the Ceiling* will find the same.

I am equally grateful to William Thompson, Warren Motte, Mark Polizzotti, and Eleanor Hardin, for their helpful and sympathetic readings of this translation. And, in particular, I thank Éric Chevillard, himself, both for his patience and good humor in responding to my many questions and doubts, and for the simple pleasure of reading and translating a text as stubbornly surprising as this one.

JORDAN STUMP

ON THE CEILING

1/1

The thickest clouds are gray, the tallest, mightiest cities are gray, the elephant, the hippopotamus, all the pachyderms are gray; they can be seen from a much greater distance than the garish hummingbird or butterfly, and yet the prejudice persists that gray is the most minimal manifestation of visibility, the least distinguishable from nothing or the closest to it, a prejudice so tenacious that it has left the masses blind: how many men, how many women go for days, months, whole years at a stretch without seeing an elephant, a hippopotamus, as if to them these enormous beasts had in fact become imperceptible? Only the occasional aesthete blessed with a musician's soul shows any real sensitivity to gray nowadays. Such creatures understand that gray comes in no fewer shades than the more straightforward colors and that each shade corresponds perfectly to one of those colors, expressing its every quality but with greater delicacy, greater authenticity, with unfailing precision and purity. Thus there is a gray equivalent of red, more subtly red than red, appearances notwithstanding, delving deeper into the idea or emotion of red than red itself, a gray redder than red, more intimately red than red, the gray of the rhinoceros for instance, a gray more clearly blue than blue, the gray of the elephant, a gray more profoundly green than green, the gray of the hippopotamus, a gray yellow in a way that yellow can never hope to be, the gray of stone. The quietly elegant among us have grasped this.

Every day, from head to toe, I dress in gray, and yet when I go out, people turn their heads and watch me pass by, they stare at me in wonder. The same gaze that overshoots the elephant, passes straight through the rhinoceros, and bounces off the hippopotamus, that same gaze falls directly on me. People notice me, I stand out. I have a very ordinary face, without beauty or ugliness. Indeed, for me a mirror is only money thrown out the window; my twins walk the streets on the other side of the glass. Of my nose, if despite myself I were forced to refine this portrait, I would say that it is home to my sense of smell; of my eyes, that without them I would find it difficult to see. All my sensory antennae are in their allotted place. I'm a good likeness; I might easily be mistaken for another, any number of others, anyone at all. And yet I hear whispering around me when I go out, and passersby point their fingers at me. When I enter some public place, a shop, a restaurant, stooping slightly as I pass through the doorway – not that I'm particularly tall, but I always wear a chair upside down on my head, and I'm afraid I might hit the doorframe or break the glass – conversation comes to a halt, then gives way to those whispers once again. I thought I'd left them outside, but clearly they're following me, like those fat houseflies that move from room to room with us, attracted by who knows what, what effluvia, apparently seeking out our company for the sole purpose of satisfying their mysterious need to annoy.

✳

I wish I could say, it would be a lie, that I was born this way, with a chair upside down on my head. But in fact the origin of the thing goes back to a time so distant that I can scarcely remember what came before. I was a fearful child, no less a loner than the crustiest codger, so unsociable that the world around me seemed to be composed entirely of third persons – to me, my fellow man was primarily, before anything else, the third person who inevitably comes along when he isn't wanted. When those around me turned their attention to me, I always felt as though I'd been snatched away from myself, cleaned out, emptied of my substance, taken over by a shaft of stares whose convergence constituted the sole proof of my presence in the world: those eyes fixed on me were the only living flesh I could still lay claim to, my very consciousness melded with the network of impressions and judgments I had inspired. Only after many long minutes alone with myself could I recompose my identity. I came back to my senses, but, for the duration of the scrutiny, I had ceased to exist, living only inasmuch as one recently deceased goes on living in the contradictory memories of his close and vague acquaintances. I dreaded nothing so much as other people's attention, which I nevertheless found impossible to escape since my reserve, mistaken for wisdom, was held up as an example for the other children who hid themselves more skillfully than I behind capers and hullabaloo. I wanted only to shrink, just as I was reaching the age when your marrow spurts like sap, when your thyroid gland rips you apart from inside; my solution was to curl up, to grow circularly, in a spiral. My mother consulted a doctor whose orders were that I wear a chair upside down on my head, an exercise that would force me to grow straight. Up I stood. So there was a place for me under the sun after all. Better yet: thus equipped, I had permanently saved myself a seat.

*

I'm settled in quite comfortably up in the heavens. I sit with the gods of legend above the clouds, among the lightning bolts, I mill the grain to bring the rain, I blow hot and cold. In short, I'm on top of things. I look down on it all. I have to stoop to see the birds, they're larger than the people. The people live far below, away at the very bottom, I can just make them out, flattened by foreshortening, their feet playing with their heads as with a ball, pushing it forward – a rapid succession of brief dribbles and hooks – dodging adversaries who likewise endeavor only to find a way around the oncomer, every man for himself, to each his own goal, I watch this endless match dispassionately, cheering neither for one side nor for another. I never take my eyes off it, but only because I have such a good seat, so comfortable, offering me a unique perspective. I never lose hope that something surprising might happen, it's rare, but sometimes a head rolls just a little too far.

*

1/5

To my knowledge, no one before me has worn a chair upside down on his head as I do, or, if so, only for short distances – but, at the same time, it would seem that no one has avoided it altogether, that is, that everyone has tried it at least once, that it would be impossible to find even one adult male who has never worn a chair upside down on his head, impossible to cite even one example, proving that this ambition lives in each of us, deep-seated, proving also that it is no easy thing to stay true to such a dream and to surrender oneself for any length of time to the sacrifices it implies, so much so that, in the end, people simply abandon it and put down the chair after a few minutes, a few yards. I'm the first to keep it up.

In crowds I am continually ogled. I attract indignant commentary because I do not relinquish my chair to an old woman growing weary or feeling poorly from standing too long – old women growing weary or feeling poorly form the greater part of the throngs in which I find myself – and in order to escape a lynching, I'm forced to come up with some sort of justification – this chair is fragile, worm-eaten, dangerous, I'm taking it to be repaired, the lady is better off tottering atop her own two legs. And I offer my services, I come forward to support the invalid, I hook her over my arm and walk her home. Never have I seen an open-air event through to the end.

But I am ashamed of these craven lies – do I owe an

explanation to anyone who asks? By what right should I be obligated to justify my conduct, to provide, as I do in this case, some pretext thanks to which others might accept my behavior? Especially since I would never hesitate to offer my chair for a few moments to an old woman who wanted to wear it on her head, who suddenly felt the imperious need to wear it on her head, to whose assistance I alone would be able to come, I alone among all these people staring balefully at me; there would be no point in her looking to any of them for help in such circumstances, one would do well to remember that.

*

Another problem: I have to stoop to get through a doorway. No accommodation has been made for us. Ceilings are often too low. Garments pulled on over the head are designed with ridiculously narrow openings at the neck. Architects and tailors seem to think we don't exist. It would never occur to them to approach their task with our special needs in mind, to take us into account; their creations are intended for the majority, and it's no concern of theirs if we can't fit through their cat-flaps. Their aim is success among the masses, we're not worth a second thought. Their indifference cuts me to the quick. What if I, seeking revenge, seeking justice in other words, what if I decided to direct my efforts only toward those of my own kind, how would I be judged? Giving up for good on speaking to the collective, on working for the benefit of the community, what if I took as my goal the satisfaction of those who wear a chair upside down on their heads, and them alone, what would people say of me? That I'm not a team player, that I preach to the converted, that I place a greater value on the approval of the elite than on popular recognition; and my works would be called esoteric, they'd be seen as decadent little curiosities at best, at worst as abstruse, pretentious parables.

I'm not a vindictive person. I can do without these low reprisals. Besides, they would only backfire. As I have said, I'm not even allowed to give tit for tat: I am permitted to bemoan my fate, nothing more, in fact that's precisely what they expect of me, they have vast stores of compassion at the ready if only I would agree to lament my situation – but without making demands, careful now, never make demands, leave the initiative to them. What they're after is an opportunity to display their beneficence. I could offer them the sweet, cozy satisfaction of finding themselves more big-hearted than they thought, more sensitive to others' distress, not as stony as they thought, and they would immediately seek to apply their generosity to me, not because they're in any way grateful, but only because they have no other means of deriving pleasure from it. It would be a clumsy generosity, of course; they would shower me with useless gifts – a hat, a comb – but all the same, should I have the audacity to resist it, to refuse its favors, should I dare to suggest that it be directed not here but there – would I not then open myself to comparison with a patient who asks only that the doctor confirm his own diagnosis and directs him to cut open his stomach in order to treat his migraines? Oh, that unexpected gush of goodness would go cold in a hurry. That great surge of generosity would vanish into thin air.

In any case, there's been a misunderstanding. I'm not unhappy with my lot. To feel pity is only to think yourself shielded from pity, or, even more perversely, it's a twisted form of envy – after all, every long-distance flight is full of double amputees who paid for their ticket with the money they've saved on shoes, while the rest of us have no choice but to stay stuck where we are, not enough money, and not enough legs either, to go and spend our vacations on the Sun as they do; we get postcards from them, along with staggering shoe-repair bills. There are advantages to my situation as well. I'm not blind to that. I don't want pity – and if I did, I could easily pity myself, I've learned to make do with what I have, a regular Robinson Crusoe – but I believe I have earned the right to ask for certain allowances: I'd like to be able to wear something other than smocks or garments that button down the front, I'd like to be able to climb into a car that's not a convertible, or use public transport. I ask only to blend in, and my way is blocked. And then people point at me, look there, another pathetic fool who'll do anything for attention. That's what I hear all around me. Know, then, that I derive from my lot less glory than humiliation; I must bow down in public buildings and government offices, where my submissive air encourages delusions of omnipotence among the most insignificant, ineffectual, and stunted desk jockeys, already overly inclined to believe that people are lining up just for a glimpse of them, although it is true that one can find in such places the last of the bearded ladies and some very remarkable two-headed pigs. My requirements are simple. I ask only that the ceilings be raised a little.

How can I explain this? The turmoil inside me, the agonizing embarrassment, the dismay I feel in the presence of any person, male or female, who is not wearing a chair upside down on his or her head. I know from experience, of course, that such encounters are still possible, probable, even quite common, but no matter how I try to anticipate them, no matter how I try to prepare myself in advance, they never fail to stun. I have few principles, I always strive to keep an open mind and to respect the choices of others, but I can't help but flinch when I meet someone who isn't wearing a chair upside down on his or her head; something inside me is profoundly disturbed, and that something, I must admit – although my devotion to good taste and harmonious geometric balance is also offended – is of a moral nature. I am aggrieved, insulted, I cannot help but see it as a serious act of provocation (as nudity in churches is, I believe, for others), a sacrilegious wantonness, and I have to force myself not to scream vilifications at the wretch, and even to lash out physically, for I have no doubt that I would be capable of violence in such moments. But I keep hold of myself, so far I've always managed to keep hold of myself: my lip trembles, my fists clench, I continue on my way.

I sometimes walk down the street where all the restaurants are, and nothing pains me quite so much as the sight of those people in the windows, sitting at their tables – alone, in couples, whole families, old married folk, widowers, all seated – pains or amuses me, it depends, all those identical toads hunched over their plate of appetizers, their pizza, or some other such lily-pad. One of them catches sight of me. Word spreads. Heads are raised. They stop chewing or carry on absent-mindedly. They watch me. Clearly, I've made an impression. That's some consolation. I like to think that they're asking themselves some hard questions at this point, that they now see themselves as they are, by way of contrast, and that they are judging themselves harshly. They were in the dark. Let them reconsider their very existence, courageously, and let them decide forthwith to transform it. They will rise up, as one, from one end to the other of the street where the restaurants are, behind every plate-glass window, grasp their chairs and don them.

*

I am trying to convert Méline; tall women are the fashion at the moment, and Méline is not indifferent to changing fashions. I'm doing my best to take advantage of that weakness. Instead of hoisting yourself up atop those high heels, atop those soles thicker than you are (how long has it been since you've walked on the ground? I miss you), come back to Earth, next to me, come on down, I'm waiting for you, I'll show you a better way to grow taller without ever leaving your neighborhood. Méline smiles. She always smiles. Her mouth smiles just as a boat floats.

Deep, black, deep black, her eyes will never see the real

beauty of the world until the one can gaze rapturously into the other.

Who would dare be so snotty as to speak of Méline's nose? It would be an injustice – would you like someone introducing you to someone else to grasp you by the nose? Besides, how can we use the word *nose*, simply *nose*, hooked but not crooked, to name the little penchant for philosophical reading that forms one of the noblest features of Méline's face?

Her ears, I whisper into them, are still or already music itself; a Chinese brush would botch the tracing of their arabesque; only the wrist of a seven-year-old violin prodigy might be able to turn it.

Méline piles her fine, frizzy hair atop her head and ties it there, and with it the thread of smoke from her cigarette, and this fluid chignon, light as a cloud, is no doubt the best way to dot the *i* that is the luminous line of her face, since a second pretty little pointed chin would surely be out of place here. But the pinewood chair I have reserved for her would be even more becoming.

    *

It was evening, and I'd been out walking for a long time. I was staggering slightly. I must have looked tired. She very sweetly offered to help carry my chair – did I live far from here? – and I had to explain. She seemed surprised but interested. She asked me why.

This was my answer: when in centuries to come historians examine our age, they will see it all with perfect clarity, the overarching structure, the fundamental axes, the turning points, the ruptures, the motivations and goals, the causes of our errors, the sources of the conflicts, the direction of the progress; of everything that seemed absurd, incoherent, they will reveal the ineluctable logic, nothing will be left to chance, coincidences that leave us nonplussed will reveal themselves for what they are: evidence, evidence proving that everything intersects and holds together. The enigma that I constitute today will be solved without delay – and as one could easily have predicted, there appeared at that juncture a man who wore a chair upside down on his head, that's what they'll say, or else: it would have been surprising, given these circumstances, if there had not then appeared a man wearing a chair upside down on his head, or: the inevitable happened, a man appeared who wore a chair upside down on his head, or: it need hardly be added that a man then appeared who wore a chair upside down on his head . . . that's what they'll say. That's what I told her. She listened to me, smiling. A woman was smiling at me and not mocking me (two incisors overlap slightly in the middle of her smile, as if jockeying for position, but so gracefully that Méline might quite legitimately lay claim to both the spangled leotard and the renown of Angélique Chiarini, Virginie Kenebel,

Ellen Kremzow, Zora Truzzi, Lily Strepetow, May Wirth, or Ella Bradna, the most elegant circus equestriennes ever to mount a white horse). She agreed to walk me home.

But we were nearly there, and I stretched out the remaining distance by crossing and recrossing streets, from one sidewalk to the other. Méline found this strange. I confessed, but not straightforwardly, that such was indeed the ruse I had chosen to keep her with me as long as possible: did you know that in the beginning snakes moved forward in a perfectly straight line, like an arrow? That's a story Madame Stempf tells her children; a remarkable woman, I'll introduce you to her. The snakes best equipped for life were the fastest. They reached their prey ahead of the rest. Left behind, the slower ones had constantly to change course in their search for food. They looked to the left, to the right, albeit never leaving the path traced by their betters – who seemed to know just what route to take in order to succeed in life – they zigzagged this way and that (they snaked, I would say if I were less loath to commit an anachronism, since at that time *to snake* still signified *to speed straight ahead like an arrow*, the authority of the strongest prevailing as it always does), until this sinuous slither began to come naturally to them; it later saved them from extinction, when, during a prolonged food shortage, the snakes that moved straight ahead like arrows continued on their witless way directly into a desert where they became lost, starved, and, one last time, left behind a lifeless skin, with no further molt to come save necrosis. Fortune smiled on the other snakes, though, who fed copiously on field mice and baby birds fallen from the nest – prosperity is always to be found just around the corner. Méline seemed to be having some difficulty following me, but I knew what I was doing: with my every sudden turn, caught unawares, she collided with me – I only had to open my arms.

*

Additionally, my chair protects me from the plaster or girders that often fall about me. I am not the only inhabitant of the trailers that sit in this abandoned work site. A library was to have been built here, I'm told. They didn't get very far with the construction. Some concrete pillars have sprouted, more or less at random, it would seem (this is what the Parthenon would look like if it had grown up in the forest), four of them still supporting a half-collapsed metallic structure. A few other traces remain of the activity that went on here for seven or eight weeks: a pile of sand already being eaten away by dirt and invaded by weeds and garbage, wonderfully sharp fossil imprints of the dorsal spines of triceratopses and tyrannosauruses left in the mud by truck tires and bulldozer treads (only a paleontologist would doubt their authenticity), here and there, still, shovels, pickaxes, lying flat, upright, other abandoned tools, trowels, sledgehammers, buckets, or, leaning against a low wall, a portable cement mixer that will never finish vomiting up its gray gruel, cold, petrified; but this last is in fact the work of my neighbor and friend Kolski, a symbol, he says, of a civilization grown sick of itself, repulsed to the point of nausea, and that has finally given up on everything it stands for: its dream of planet-wide urbanization turns to upset stomach in a distant corner of a vacant lot. Kolski's work is born of long reflection; it is founded on an uncompromising political analysis that later serves, quite logically, as its most astute interpretation. Having arrived at these conclusions, with the confident execution characteristic of a lucid creator inhabited by a great idea, Kolski gathered up his strength and set to work: with one push he leaned the cement mixer up against the little wall.

After two months of work, when the excavators had leveled the terrain and the crews hired to build the foundations had only just taken over from them, the construction of the library was suspended by order of the public authorities, along with, I suppose, I hope, all literary projects then underway – for under the circumstances, what could be done with newly published works, where could they be shelved, classified, catalogued, listed, and then forgotten, where to warehouse them, how to get them out of the way? Unless, of course, it was a sudden mass resignation of writers – because what's the point of writing? – that brought about the suspension of the work. Architecturally, the project was an ambitious one: the library was to have covered seven hectares, encircling a little woods (perhaps an ornamental Forest of Arden, perhaps a raw supply of paper pulp – might this unlikely threat have caused the trees, even though sheltered from the wind, to tremble just a little?), ringed with two levels of galleries and four right-angled glass towers 80 meters high, housing 395 kilometers of shelves, whereas a good reader covers at most 150 meters of printed pages over his entire existence, donning glasses after a few dozen meters naked-eyed, gripping an enormous magnifying glass for the last meter. That would have been an excellent argument for the abandonment of the project – who would ever be so foolish as to embark on a voyage knowing full well that they will never make it to the end, that they will in fact die having just set off? But the argument was never made. Workers and technicians were taken off the job without explanation; they were needed to dig highways lengthwise and crosswise, or stadiums in circles, projects bespeaking a more enlightened sense of public utility. They didn't even bother to take away the sheds, the storage buildings of undulating sheet metal, and the prefabricated bungalows that served as offices for the crew foremen. Padlocks were hung on the front doors of all those little houses.

    *

Strong padlocks, too: for those without a key ring, a pickaxe is the key that fits such locks best. Smashed forcefully against the lock several times, it soon penetrates the secret mechanism; the chain falls away and the door slips aside before you as if opened from within by a loving spouse; your favorite dish is simmering on the stove, your three little girls leap into your arms, the family dog greets you tenderly, you step inside, pushing along toward the back of the shelter the bags of sand and cement blocking your way, you clear away various obstructions, the wheelbarrow, the boards, the tools, the buckets, then you sweep the trash-strewn floor, and the last thing you throw out the door, the filthiest piece of garbage in the pile, is a rotting straw broom – thus, first among us, Topouria made himself at home.

A crane operator on the construction site, he was unable to find another job when the project was halted, and he went into business for himself, but not as a crane operator, no surprise there, although he excelled in the exercise of that delicate art and was one with his machine to such an extent that he could easily have blended into a herd of giraffes without awakening their suspicion, feeding as they do on tender leaves ripped one by one from the highest branches of the trees, gracefully kneeling for a drink of water, effortlessly seducing a female thanks to the refinement of his approach, his thoughtfulness, his distinguished air, his good looks, his discreetly elegant ways, his tact, his great gentleness – and so precise, too: he operated his machine with such finesse that when you saw him hoisting stones into the sky you found yourself thinking he was hanging the stars out for the night. What a man for the crane! It was not by chance that Topouria's resolute mind had allied itself with that immense body, docile, built for raising and razing mountains, and equally capable of pulling a speck of dust from your eye with its iron jaws. Topouria had the world at his feet. No longer did his brain command only four puny limbs; a motor now relayed his every directive, a steel shaft extended his every bone: he had what it took to have things his way. His gaze carried far, dazzling despite the filthy windows of the operator's cabin, virtually impossible to stare down. His gestures were slow, unstoppable, imbued with all the solemnity of a master chess player.

Unfortunately he never had the chance to show what he was capable of, but his plans for a general reorganization of things got around; after work on the library had been suspended, his crew was invited to participate in the construction of a bridge, and Topouria immediately devised a plan to build it parallel to the river's axis, thereby allowing the latter to step over the ocean and continue its way on the thirsty, infertile continent that lies stretched out on the other side. Once he'd got wind of this, the head foreman chose to send him packing. Topouria saw the great paralyzed carcass of his crane glide away on its prosthetic wheels, an excruciating amputation – even today he retains the sensations and reflexes of the mighty body that once was his, and this brings him many frustrations: he believes he is capable of lifting loads which are clearly too heavy for him, and he makes himself look ridiculous trying to straighten or topple walls that to his great astonishment resist him, first time this has happened. But Topouria will not let himself be discouraged. His former vigor will return, he's sure of it, just as soon as he gets some rest. He sells scrap metal he finds on the work site, biding his time until he has completely regained his health and can resume his activities and return to his project, sometimes testing his strength, pushing against a wall or a pillar, without much success; they never move. First Madame Stempf, then Malton and Lanson, Kolski, and finally myself, we all joined him here, and there is still space available for new tenants in the other trailers.

Madame Stempf could never bring herself to part with her children, two or three, maybe four; her concept of maternity views obstetrics as a forced eviction at the hands of unfeeling brutes who, when faced with the slightest resistance, have no qualms about clamping their pincers over human fetuses no more than nine months old, before they're done, their bones still too green, too flexible, their brain incapable of a single witticism, even spread on a cracker it would make a sad sort of appetizer. Our friend wasn't about to let her children be taken from her that way, she kept them within herself, tucked away, her four or five children, maybe six, spreading her stomach around them and erecting the rampart of her body against the cold of winter, against the night, against the wind, against the storm, against rusty nails, fingernails, elbows, hooks, against blades, bullets, blows – they were quite at home there, lulled by the slow roll of her enormous hips, of her immeasurable bust, they thrived: sometimes the undulating movements of those dear large angels can be made out beneath her dress. Madame Stempf stuffs herself with sweets and cakes for them – she swallows anything that might give them merriment in fact, little celluloid toys or Christmas wreaths, and the painful contractions that then torment her from deep in her entrails she delightedly attributes to the surge of joy that her gifts have aroused, to the children's excitement, all absorbed in their new games.

To keep them from boredom – for the rampart of her body is powerless against boredom, against that one formidable woe that is boredom, anterior to everything on Earth, anterior to life itself, in which might lie the origin of life's desperate emergence amid the silence and the stillness, each of them intolerable to the other, a sudden discharge born of the tension of their relationship like a bolt of lightning flashing through the leaden sky, life, as unexpected and yet as inevitable as the little mouse that suddenly springs from a solid wall, and boredom, blown off its throne, has been laying endless traps for us ever since, hoping to take it back, and still today our only weapons against it are noise and movement – she dances for them, with them, in place, she jumps from one foot to the other or spins around, at tremendous speed, arms spread, an airy dance, carried away by the weight of her ample body, a sail floating above the sea; airy in a way unknown to all those emaciated bodies that have offered themselves up to the dance and consumed themselves within it: the spirit of the dance, garrotted by muscle, confined in a prison of bone, finds its freedom in Madame Stempf, rejoices, stirring up that flesh like so much smoke, with the merest gesture one momentary statue crumbles and gives way to another, just as lovely, just as worthy of immortality, which unmakes itself at once, and so without surcease, along the narrow line of equipoise marches a procession of undreamt-of figures, impossible to pin down, to recreate, and finally Madame Stempf, exhausted, falls back onto her chair and all at once grows still again, unshakable, hands flat on her belly, the better to feel her delighted children still whirling and frolicking under the influence of the speed, their arms outstretched, then they grow calm in turn.

Next Madame Stempf sings to them, all the while repairing the straw seats on her chairs, in a slightly gravelly voice, the old repertoire of nonsense rhymes and lullabies; they fall asleep. She speaks to them as well, at great length, she instructs them, in the morning she gives them lessons in history or algebra, dreary inventories of numerical operations in either case, she teaches them fables, when bedtime comes she tells them beautiful stories, such as: a princess was despondent over her inability to find a husband, she went into the dark forest to consult the witch who in exchange for three hairs from her head confided that she had put a curse on the handsomest man in the land, the proudest and the most valiant, because he had refused her favors: with a single kiss to the ugly toad that he had become, the princess could break the spell. A great hunt was organized throughout the kingdom, the hunters would be given a golden coin for every toad brought back alive. All the toads in the land were captured, then conveyed by the cartload to the castle and the waiting princess, who, overcoming her disgust, set out to kiss the hideous creatures one by one. A month went by, and from morning 'til night, the princess kissed the toads presented to her on a red velvet pillow by a servant who then flung them into a stinking incinerator, for the magic wasn't happening: the toads shrank back in horror as the princess's little pink mouth brushed their pustulated backs; toads they remained, and so the servant dumped them from the pillow into the flames until, at last, only two were left. But no sooner had the princess's lips touched the first of the two than he metamorphosed into a prince, limpid of gaze, blond of hair, tall of body, who tenderly clasped her to him as the last toad was released into the castle's pond, aside which in later years the princess, now a queen, often came to sit and dream, gently waving her long red scarf over the water.

*

In those days, I was rooming with Kolski in an unused refrigerated warehouse, and nearly every day, from our window, we saw Madame Stempf pass by, walking along the river, slow and hurried, ponderous and vaporous, like a cloud hanging low on the horizon, reshaped from moment to moment, now compacting itself into a solid mass, now ballooning anew and expanding in all directions, never ceasing to be itself nor blending into another, its visible form, moreover, never occupying the entire volume of space available to it and so inseparable from it, like the conjunction of a wooden panel and a semi-circle of emptiness that constitutes an open or closed door. A ray of light broke through that cloud: Madame Stempf was on her way home again, a bale of rushes or rattan tucked under her arm, and the sight of those long golden stems made me yearn for still waters, for lazy afternoons on stream banks, and then she disappeared, taking the scenery with her; suddenly I was standing once more before a muddy river, like a vacationer who has been taken in by the brochure promoting a seaside village and scurries over the dunes, pulling on his large, flowered swim trunks, only to find himself mired amid a clutch of black, viscous seagulls, the pigeons on the quay were standing idly. My disappointment was short-lived. I had happened upon a magnificent character: beyond all doubt, this beautiful creature, laden with reeds, was a chair caner – I would be needing her.

It's not hard to see why: people in my profession work sitting down, only work sitting down. You can stand up, of course, it's not forbidden, walk around a bit, pace aimlessly for a moment, often that clears things up, reveals new perspectives, some new way out of the problem, but you have to sit again if you want to proceed through that exit. You can also lie down for a few minutes, the enervation fades, suddenly you clearly see the goals to be pursued, and with them the obvious truth that you will never attain them flat on your back, you have to sit again. Only by sitting down can you hope to get somewhere in this line of work. Not only the quantity but also the quality of the product depend on our ability to sit for hours at a time.

When I am sitting, the back of the chair I wear upside down on my head meets the back of my desk chair, forming a narrow wooden cell – a confessional, a guardhouse – perfectly suited to my work: I am thereby twice as efficient as anyone else in the business, I tackle twice the workload in the same amount of time, and the result is twice as satisfactory in every way. I wouldn't make much of a runner (except in my own very specific category, where I have no serious competition), nor much of a high jumper, diver, dancer (save in matched competitions, with all contenders similarly equipped), but when it comes to the exercise of this profession, there is none better suited than I.

Of course I also wear out twice as many chairs as my competitors. The wooden skeleton holds up nicely, but the cane or straw seat soon weakens, no less the one on which I sit for hours on end, restless, rolling from one buttock to the other as I cross and uncross my legs, sometimes bouncing up and down a little to stretch my muscles or out of impatience, than the one hanging over me, whose delicate canework my very hard and slightly pointed skull indents a little more deeply with every bounce (an action particularly destructive when caused by merriment), and which is further abraded by simple friction, just as a hat wears thin even on a cool head. At one time I made a point of alternating chairs every day, crowning myself with the one I was sitting on the day before, and vice versa, for I supposed that the chair supporting the weight of my body must age more quickly, but I was soon forced to rethink this idea: I kept my chair on my head from morning to night, but I never worked for more than three or four hours at a time, so the process of destruction, speedier but irregular in the one case, slower but continual in the other, was in the end identical; they differed only in their manner and their rhythm.

I owned many chairs, in every style, and I took pleasure in changing them often, according to the season or simply on a whim. Some, with wooden seats, were all but impervious to my fidgeting or bouncing but uncomfortable and endowed with a sort of group instinct at odds with my own aspirations; I sensed their eagerness to fall into line, to form rows, and I, myself, no matter how I fought it, fell back into the schoolchild's posture, detrimental to my work, paralyzing, I avoided them whenever possible. As for my tapestry chairs, relegated to a corner of the bedroom, the seats were all torn or unraveling, they looked like emaciated old donkeys with their mouths full of hay, they were of no use to me. And, in any case, I've always preferred cane, rattan, wicker, or jute to wood or cloth, for their flexibility, their elasticity, and the softness that comes with it, and also because they conform to my idea of the chair's essence, aesthetically and philosophically speaking, the genius of nature and the industry of man coming together to conceive and construct this modest household object: a small tree with an easily accessible nest. But the ten or twelve chairs I then owned with seats of straw or cane, all damaged in one way or another, were in urgent need of repair; what a coincidence, a caner walked by my window every day.

*

A sliding meat hook suspended from a rod on the ceiling served as our communal coat rack, but Kolski often hung from it himself, by his feet, from dawn to dusk. Ideas came to him more freely this way, he said. He liked to feel his blood in a dense clump between his temples. The extensile movements of our arms and legs betray our great weakness; our mind, embarrassed and ashamed, wants nothing to do with our body, and so we try to keep our distance from the body, or rather we push it away from us, roughly, as far from us as possible we fling its tattered shreds, handfuls of flesh and bone: all day long the wretch reels, shaken by kicks and punches, finally collecting himself, only to collapse into mindless slumber – dreams themselves are only games of the mind in which our body is not allowed to join; if it makes the occasional little movement, or little sound, it's only because it's bored or creaking in solidarity with the bedstead. Kolski had chosen to stop running. In fact, he found his self-imposed visits to the interior of his body quite pleasant, he said, after fifteen painful minutes of apoplexy. He conceived many of his works in abstract form during these sessions, effortlessly, he worked out the means of bringing them to fruition – because the whole of my oxygenated thought is contained in my head, he explained, not dispersed throughout my limbs, overseeing and informing my every movement, busily taking note of the sensations transmitted by my nerves and reacting accordingly, all those little chores that ordinarily take up its time and keep it from its meditations: our thought escapes us the moment we move, it runs through our restless fingers, whereas contemplation does not similarly deprive us of our body; I feel mine existing more clearly than ever in my hours of dizzy prostration above the ground, my ankylosis, thrumming and pricking, keeps me apprised of my orientation in space, I know just where I am, outlined like a shadow on a wall and entirely absorbed in myself, like the animals in the butcher's window whose final state I thus lucidly experience, deriving a rich understanding of this final state, which is furthermore no less central to the happiest years of their lives, wholly oriented toward the hook that awaits them, that great hook buried deep in the hay, in the green sunshine of the meadows, in all that is their feast and festivity, and it is deeply rewarding to perceive the destiny of the cow better than any cow could, to be the first enlightened cow. Let us first try to solve the small mysteries if we want to penetrate the enigmas of our own condition. Let us begin by educating the cow within us. How else can we ever hope that some gleam of intelligence might one day flicker to life in the bovine stare with which we contemplate such vital questions?

*

I first met Kolski in the waiting room of a train station, at rush hour, with the seats all taken and a crowd of people standing, staggering from exhaustion, staring at my upside-down chair with equal parts desire and condemnation, hastily sealing a pact against me with an exchange of glances, like lynchers looking for a mob. And yet there were a number of empty seats at the far end of the room on a bench where a man, alone, curled up under his overcoat, seemed to be sleeping; it was Kolski, he stank like a sewer and I took shelter in his odor, a safe haven, protecting me as securely as bulletproof glass from the hostile crowd, which had no choice but to keep its distance, impotent against me. I made Kolski's odor my own, so strong, so overpowering an odor that the two of us could easily share custody of it. Not only did he and I have ten or twelve seats to ourselves in this crowded room, but, more than that, I was wearing a chair on my head, and, more than that, our stench was repelling our enemies, squeezing them, jamming them up against each other. I was thoroughly enjoying the moment, why not admit it? We stood at the center of a broad empty circle, our persons respected on all sides despite the crowd's contemptuous airs, masters of all we surveyed within range of the miasma emanating from Kolski's clothes and body. For once I was on the winning side. Kolski stank, and I stank with him, wholeheartedly. Whenever he moved in his sleep, the invisible, fetid cloud enveloping us took wing, waves of seaweed and dead fish crested slowly, then suddenly crashed over our victims: their faces grew long, yellower, their nostrils pinched, their eyes half shut, as if those apertures, too, had to be sealed off against a smell as penetrating as this and as inseparably intertwined with light; some were taken ill, there were faintings, finally the mob sounded the retreat. This defensive stench to which I almost certainly owed my life was thus no less fearsome a weapon in counterattack, and easily deployed, no need even to brandish it, and with it at our side what empire could we not have conquered, what vast domains for our celebrations, for our unholy pleasures and our games – I sat alone with Kolski in the deserted waiting room.

He awoke. Silently I held out half my sandwich – do not misunderstand me: I didn't offer him one of the two slices of bread that constitute a sandwich, I had genuinely split my sandwich in two, performing what stratigraphers, evoked here for a good reason, call a cross section, revealing a basal sediment of wheat flour, salt, yeast, and butter, the latter deposited after the rest but today almost completely assimilated into the crumb, then a very thin leaf of lettuce, itself overlaid by an extraordinarily fine and translucent slice of ham, no doubt carved from the virtuous soul of a piglet, whose unexpected presence thus suddenly revealed was in itself justification enough for this stratigraphical analysis, which now comes to a close along with its object, the final stratum consisting, like the first, of a stale aggregate of flour, salt, and yeast – Kolski opened wide and engulfed it all – in his half was a fossilized pickle, I owed him that.

We became friends. He took an interest in me, in my unusual way of occupying a chair, but not out of idle curiosity, he himself had always thought, he said, that chairs were not being put to the best possible use, relegated to desk jobs, limited to the rather degrading function of seats, excluded from any other sort of employment, he was sure they must have something more to offer us than that, that there must be a better way to show our appreciation for their perfect forms than by pressing our butts against them, yet until now he'd never known how to flesh out this vague suspicion. I had given him the solution. I'd rescued him from a difficult moral dilemma – from then on, he often accompanied me on my errands and daily strolls, wearing a nice lyre-backed chair I'd loaned him. One fine day, we even went out under a little wicker bench, very light, built for two: it was as if we were walking along beneath a mother's tender gaze, I had discovered the meaning of fraternity, its synchronized footsteps, its doubled breath, its doubled furrow, and its wide turns beneath the yoke.

I in turn inquired into Kolski's activities. They were to be found in the field of art, more precisely they set out to broaden the field of art, so as to finally find a way out of it, to annex all other fields to it by assimilation, seduction, contagion, digestion, guerilla occupation. All other fields, Kolski explained to me, politics, economics, religion, are only metaphysical systems dreamed up by our heavy brains, which float in the air, held fast to the heavens, thanks only to a fistful of hair. Blind and deaf, our feet have lost contact with us. A fog rising from the mud, such is nature to man, prisoner that he is to a depressing, harsh, and violent dream, which he mistakes for reality – it's all in his head. His imagination alone swathed the king in an ermine robe lined with the same animal's blood, it created an order in which the arbitrary forms of the merchant, the accountant, the military or religious tyrant can be made out. The artist can feel only scorn for this false prestige, bestowed by the imagination, which allows the farce to go on. He must first of all give himself a good pinch so as to return to his senses: the body fortunately never leaves them – despite its frequent periods of numbness, seemingly embalmed or mummified alive, it remains capable of healthy reactions. Kolski had made the decision to trust only in the body. His current project was the odor of men. We don't know what it is, he told me. We perfume, wash, soap our body, in an attempt to hold it in check, to immobilize it, as if we fear, and rightly so perhaps, that its odor might usurp the place of our thought. Deodorized, our body is bound hands and feet, kept to itself, circumscribed by its outline, it won't get far. It will never prosper, will never expand. We die precisely where we were born. Kolski had given up bathing, determined not to hinder his growth, curious to see where it might take him – and the fact that the smell of men, when allowed to thicken, to expand, to unfold in space, turns out to be somewhat disagreeable, and indeed suffocating, didn't bother him, on the contrary he hoped that it might soon become dense enough, compact enough, solid enough for his sculptor's hands to make something of it. Already he had plans for a great work, richly colored, light, indestructible, which he would call *Springtime*. He also informed me that his landlord had tossed him out, that he'd spent the past month hanging around this train station, and since it was lonely in my cold room, I offered to put him up. Once he was there, he took a shower and moved on to other experiments, of a rather different nature, quite contrary, requiring, as we have seen, the most profound concentration.

Life was very different in the Middle Ages, we collapsed onto benches or stools, our muscles relaxed all at once like rigging gone slack, they loosened their grip, our stomach caught us as we fell, the body's bony parts and fleshy parts worked together in harmony, more or less, according to the slope of the seat, so as to offer us a comfortable sit-down. We were simple people, tough and tireless at work, flabbily inert at rest. But on massive, immovable thrones with straight backs and broad headrests sat eminent ecclesiastics, no less permanent, who held us in their grip with threats and terror. That wasn't enough for them. Creatures who move on two legs are unpredictable, they may sometimes follow the same road, but they soon separate, each goes his own way. Quadrupeds, on the other hand, assemble into close-knit herds whenever possible, directed by a single will, easily steered. In this realization lies the origin of the chair. For it was thus that an unfocused, restless crowd of scatterbrained individuals was transformed into an audience, by definition attentive: a chair is a gregarious thing, it falls in alongside its fellows; unlike, for instance, the stool, it forces the human body into its own posture – what's more, it imposes a direction on the gaze, given our inability to unscrew our neck, we see of the world only what the chair shows us. Confined within a row, hemmed in among all the others, its equals, the chair becomes impossible both to move and to leave;

we have no choice but to endure the show or the lesson to the bitter end.

And so a throng of chairs was assembled and set out before the thrones of the eminent ecclesiastics, to begin with, and then the system refined and perfected itself on its own: today the child, from earliest youth, is invited to sit down and then riveted to his seat – his cries of pain or protest are drowned out by the shouts, the singing, and the applause of spectators already won over – he will not stand up again. From then on, it takes only a few barks to gather the flock together and confine it within churches, schools, movie theaters, and all the other pastures where the eminent ecclesiastics currently tend their sheep.

There have been many dissidents before me, most notably in seventeenth-century England and a century later in America; the devotees of the Windsor chair, a saddle-shaped elm seat fitted with a backrest in the form of a horseshoe, managed to break away from the pack, it didn't last, they soon turned against each other, competing amongst themselves, they wasted their energy on pointless races around tables, under the parlor wainscoting. Their rebellion ran out of steam and ended in absurdity, no doubt paving the way for the appearance, soon after, of the desk chair, with which all hope of liberation was lost: subdued, mastered, tamed, domesticated, and then yoked to a desk like a horse to a heavy cart, the last of the wild chairs were brought forever to heel. (But I would be remiss if I didn't acknowledge the willfulness that some chairs retain even today; when treated too roughly they buck and throw off their schoolchild or administrator, isolated explosions of temper or pride which so far as I know have never led to any spontaneous reaction of solidarity, and this I deeply regret, I would give up a great deal for the chance to witness a general uprising of desk chairs.)

*

The webbed seat of the Egyptians, the *sella curulis* of the Romans, and later their *cathedra* – which is also its etymon – may be considered the chair's earliest forerunners. I have studied its history, from the beginning, its evolution, speedier than any other skeleton's, I have admired the flexibility of its unchanging structure and the exceptional adaptability with which it bends to meet the requirements of every sort of etiquette without ever failing the demands of its primary function, I have travelled deep into the countryside to interview hoary artisan furniture makers, master carpenters, I have clapped my ear to the trunks of thrice-centenarian oaks from which we might even today legitimately carve authentic Louis XIV furniture, I have consulted old women who once earned their living renting out the metal armchairs in public parks (one of them had seen the writer Marcel Proust sit down, and the event remained remarkably fresh in her memory: he bent his legs until his buttocks came into contact with the seat, then relaxed his upper body until his spine was resting against the back of the chair) – the results of my research would easily fill a definitive work on the question, but that's not my purpose here. And I refuse to vulgarize a knowledge gained over many years of study under the top specialists: there are some things that everyday language cannot account for, no more than the four basic operations can express the whole of mathematics, the chair is more complicated an object than it appears, deeply implicated in the human drama; I would never forgive myself if by setting out a simplistic overview of my discoveries I confirmed the homely reputation with which it is so naively saddled.

But let us remember this at least: my chair is a cathedral. In a way I'm rather proud of that: I'm not the sort of man who walks around with a rat on his shoulder. But in spite of the distinction it bestows on me, I will never forget that the chair is first of all a cage, cleverly deconstructed, but a cage all the same, devised to leave us no choice but to listen to sermons, a stairstep pillory, the wooden body of paralysis itself lifting us onto its lap. As a child I was entrusted to a chair because I was going astray, and the chair was to straighten me out. I was on my way to becoming a hunchback, and hunchbacks are not loved, they're feared, their twisted skeleton seems all too well suited to the human soul, whose rectitude we endeavor to express with our stiff-necked postures, and which we pretend to believe is revealed only in the limpid pools of the eyes. But if I think of people I pass in the street as hunchbacks, when I imagine them as hunchbacks, I inevitably find that this little operation has made them more human: there is something lumpy, limp, and blurry about the human countenance, at once shifty and grasping, the shadow of a hump would make a perfect cover for that darkly cunning face.

And so they stood me up straight. They assumed that once cured I would overturn the corrective chair and take a seat like all the others. To be sure, I could easily grasp it by the leg or by one of the backrest's uprights, raise it, remove it from my skull, and set it on the ground, nothing could be simpler, a series of quick, uncomplicated moves – just like doffing a hat – and with that this whole affair would come to an instantaneous end. Why not? I sometimes play with the idea, gently, lovingly. I listen to it purr for a moment. Before long it rolls over onto its back, paws in the air, offering itself to my caresses – and so encourages me to hold to my original stance. It all begins again.

*

Not long after Kolski had moved in with me, I stumbled into a painful encounter: at the bend of a sidewalk, I suddenly found myself face to face with a man walking very fast, we nearly collided, he had a chair upside down on his head. We looked at each other oddly. He didn't slow down.

With long strides he hurried on his way. I realized that he was trying to get away from me. Even among my own kind, then, however few of us there are, nothing is simple, we've learned to trust no one, after a few bad experiences, we reflexively run or retreat; this man undoubtedly assumed that I was one of those occasional chair-wearers, movers, waiters, municipal employees, by the sight of whom I, too, have been deceived, believing I'd found a brother, striking up a knowingly sympathetic conversation, overjoyed to escape my solitude, only realizing my mistake when my new friend loaded the chair onto a truck or set it down before a bandstand, gestures horrible to behold, performed mechanically, coldly, as if he had no idea of their implications, and sometimes even with a snicker: his derision wounded me more deeply than his falseness.

I never saw the man with the chair again. I did look for him around the neighborhood in the days following our meeting; when I went out for a walk I headed for the street corner where we had run into each other, never losing hope that he might suddenly appear – whereupon I would introduce myself, I would clear up the misunderstanding – my gait quickened as I neared the corner. Often, in fact, since he hadn't appeared, I retraced my steps, I walked ten meters back, then started forward again as if nothing had happened, again and again I aimed my footsteps toward the exact location of our encounter, naively hoping to recreate it by replicating the conditions that had first brought it about, by sheer obstinacy and desire. One evening, in my haste – I was nearly running – I sideswiped a baby carriage, it toppled, screams rang out, I knelt over the wreckage and from it I pulled – but it was immediately snatched away from me by little clawlike hands – the lifeless body, stiff and cold, and miraculously unhurt, of a child's doll; on another occasion, I surprised a man carrying a long board over his shoulder: I had the terrifying feeling that I had arrived ahead of the event, impelled here by my impatience before the stranger's chair had been carved out and put together. I decided to return the next day and try my luck one last time.

It was then that I met Malton and Lanson: they rounded the corner at the same time as I, and so my persistence was repaid, albeit not in the way I was expecting. Lanson was pushing Malton's wheelchair, more precisely he was using it to support himself, was clinging to it to keep from falling, he depended on those two wheels for forward motion no less than his friend did. I saw in them a reflection of myself. We had many experiences in common, the same travails. I for my part had immediately earned their respect, I was doing the whole job myself, they would never have thought such a thing possible.

Lanson and Malton were coming home after a walk, I continued mine alongside them. Soon we came to a corru-

gated tin palisade, Lanson pushed aside one of the panels
and invited me in. This was where they lived, in this abandoned construction site. My gaze fell on a man bent at the
waist, as if broken in two, standing amid piles of scrap
metal and stones; feet firmly planted on the ground, he
was moving his upper body in quick semicircles, sometimes extending an arm toward an enormous beam and
trying vainly to move it – he stood upright, crestfallen,
then another piece of debris attracted his attention, and
the strange gymnastics resumed. Malton introduced me.
Topouria grasped my hand between his fingers and raised
it high in the air with evident satisfaction. He told me that
work on the enormous library that was to have been built
there had been called off without explanation almost as
soon as it had begun. The workers had all left. He'd stayed
on alone for a few weeks, and then Lanson and Malton had
joined him; they now lived in the trailers, as he did. When
I asked if there was anyone else living here, Topouria
turned his entire body in one continuous motion, never
lifting his feet from the ground, arm outstretched, and my
first thought was that he wanted me to admire the fragile
prototype of a right angle nestling in the damp jewel box
of his underarm, but then in three precise steps he operated the three articulations of his index finger and an-
swered yes, her, Madame Stempf. It was the caner – would
she be willing to rent out her skills to me? Malton didn't

doubt it, and with resolute gait, I went to see her, carefully following the path that Topouria's index finger cleared for me amid the debris – he kept his arm raised until I reached her, clearly pleased with his work.

*

Madame Stempf was sitting on the steps of her trailer, perfectly still, only her long, slender fingers were moving, as if all the accumulated energy of that massive body was channeled straight to them, they worked swiftly, surely, as supple as the stalks of rattan that they twisted and twined; she wasn't even watching them, she left them to their task, they had nothing more to learn from her. I was just about to make my request when she began to speak in a low voice, gentle, maternal, not addressed to me, and I didn't dare interrupt, hoping as I was to win her sympathy, and so I had no choice but to hear her out to the end, and this delay gave me a chance to judge the quality of her handiwork and convinced me to entrust my chairs to her.

If you want to connect two separate stories, you need a third, one that will strengthen and support the fragile web woven by the pure happenstance of the encounter – thus Madame Stempf, all the while interlacing her strips of cane horizontally, vertically, then diagonally, began the story that brought us together, for as I listened, I became one of the children for whose benefit she spoke and of whose existence I was as yet unaware, but here's the story.

A young shepherd who lived alone with his animals sensed that he was being watched whenever he led them to the river to drink. What made this particularly odd was that no one, unless by sorcery, would ever have been able to conceal themselves amid the sparse rushes along the riverbank. But one day he clearly saw two astonished eyes staring at him from the surface of the water. He jumped back so suddenly that the stranger apparently took fright and disappeared quickly into the depths of the river. Recovering from his surprise, the shepherd drew near the river again. He leaned carefully over the water, and the two eyes, warier now, were once more fixed upon him. Their gaze was that of a youthful-looking man, open and innocent, and now seemed to share in his emotion. The shepherd, fascinated, returned to the river again and again. Gradually his relationship with the stranger evolved. They smiled at each other now, without fear; sometimes they sat lost in the same inexpressible melancholy – their mated souls were unfailingly in agreement. Soon the shepherd forgot about his herd and set up camp beside the river's edge. He never left the spot until nightfall, when his friend, too, had to return beneath the water. At the first light of dawn they took their places again, and so the day passed by, their silent contemplations never interrupted. That winter was a harsh one, and the river froze solid. Something must have gone seriously wrong with the climate, in fact, for when spring returned, the temperature scarcely rose at all, the waters of the river did not thaw. But this made little difference to their daily ritual, the shepherd bundled himself up in his sheepskin, the only change he noticed was that his friend's wonderfully tender face was more unchanging now, but by this time they knew each other so well that they could express their feelings without having to display them openly. One fine day – how many seasons had gone by since the shepherd had abandoned his animals? – the king's daughter's carriage struck a root on the road alongside the river and crashed into the ditch. Her driver and her maidservant perished in the accident. In the distance, the distraught princess saw a man kneeling over the water and went to ask his help. Drawing near, she suddenly saw the man's face over his shoulder, reflected in the frozen surface of the river as in a mirror, a face she was sure she knew, so strongly did it resemble one she'd often seen in her dreams, a noble face with a steady gaze, an almost feminine mouth, a slender, fine-nostrilled nose, beautiful dark curls – and, overcome by emotion, she laid her hand on his shoulder and greeted the stranger, making no attempt to hide the quiver in her voice. Roused from his meditation, he turned to face her, she felt her heart grow cold at the sight of this cretinous old man, all scabs and grimy whiskers, his face furrowed with sinuous wrinkles, his bloodshot eyes glistening between their lids like two open wounds, his nose drooling into his mouth, he held out a hand as thin as a pincer, but she had already fled. Back at the castle, she told her father the king of her misadventure, and he sent out a squadron of soldiers from his private guard. On their return, they confessed that they had found no one, but – and this was good news for the kingdom, long awaited – they were happy to report that the thaw had finally begun, and already the river was flowing between its banks, just as it used to.

The story was over, the chair finished. Madame Stempf's agile hands fell still, like two spiders in their webs: soon someone would come along and sit here, it was inevitable, their efforts would be repaid. And I was little better than that huge insect, entangled in my words as I struggled awkwardly to formulate a suitable greeting. Finally Madame Stempf looked up at me. She eyed the chair on my head with particular attention, thinking I was bringing it in for repairs. I explained that this one, no, could wait, but I had a dozen more whose seats were completely broken through. I would very much like to leave them with her, if, that is, she would be so kind as to take on the work. That's my job, she told me, drawing a handful of chocolates from a bag and raising them to her lips, I have a family to feed.

On the theory that city dwellers deprived of a suitable re-
ceptacle for their garbage and trash would consume the fat
and bone from meat, the rinds of cheeses, the pits and peels
of fruit, appeasing their morning and evening hunger with
the same dish, that they would avoid canned food, frozen
food, all forms of processed food whose cans and wrappers
might clutter their homes, and that in this way they would
slash their food intake, and with the savings thus realized
escape their poverty, Kolski spent several weeks stealing
trash cans from the doorsteps of apartment buildings. He
brought them back to the warehouse, twelve or fifteen of
them every night, storing them first in our room and then,
when that began to fill up, in the hallways. But – apart from
the fact that one solitary man, no matter how resolute, even
if he had managed to rally to his cause a contingent of ea-
ger volunteers, could hardly hope in this way to influence
the order of things or to stand up to the power of the special interests involved – in the end, the elegant reasoning
behind his plan was foiled by the consumers' heedlessness;
they simply tossed their debris into sacks, and those sacks
pell-mell onto the sidewalk, generating more garbage than
ever, it seemed, as if up until then their trash cans' limited
volume had been holding them back: with those out of the
way, they were free to waste all the more. Kolski gave up,
but he couldn't bring himself to return the stolen trash
cans, whose stench soon became unbearable – sometimes,

in fact, one of them would begin to jiggle, then its lid would blow off under the pressure of the putrid gases fermenting inside; giant cadavers emerged, badly decomposed, already invisible, and wandered around the room, through the hallways, in search of a broken windowpane through which to make their escape, tormented souls finally reconciled with Heaven; others immediately took their place, unpleasant company.

I was once very fond of that cold room, though, whose magic still seemed to be at work long after the refrigeration systems had fallen silent; from the window, I often watched the afternoon light fade away while within my four white-tiled walls it was still as bright as early morning; the hours I spent in that room added nothing to the total of the rest, and when I stepped outside, the world seemed changed, a slightly different era, several species of animals had become extinct since my last emergence, I saw signs of fatigue on the faces of my acquaintances, sometimes they'd adopted a new style of dress or a new slang that made them seem foreign to me – I was dated, not having aged a second.

With Kolski's trash cans, corruption had come into my home, mildew flecked the grout between the tiles on the walls, a subterranean dampness hung in the room, doing irreparable harm to the straw or tapestry of my chairs, their delicate wood, warped, worm-eaten, had taken on the look of the old dead apple trees you find in abandoned or-

chards; it was time to move on. But even then I wouldn't
have dreamt of parting with those chairs, my only portable
property (so portable in fact that they had all roamed further on my two tireless legs than they ever could have on all
four of theirs, even if they did know how to gallop). Thus I
made the decision to leave this place and move into a trailer
on the library work site, next door to the caner who was to
restore my chairs. No small advantage: I wouldn't have to go
far. Because there's no denying that I look faintly ridiculous
when I carry a chair in my hand in addition to the one on
my head, I look as though I'm deliberately trying to go too
far in order to express my personal pride or my outright
contempt for the sensibilities of others, possibly straining
the patient benevolence of anyone who might at least try to
understand me: such little acts of provocation, once a favorite indulgence of mine, conceived as a slap in the face of
public opinion, whose smug authority and obtuse righ-
teousness I loathed, seeking to avenge my wounded self-
respect by feigning lightheartedness, by trying to appear so
oblivious to taunts that I intentionally brought them on
myself, not content merely to persist in my way of life, but
flaunting it, exhibiting myself everywhere with two chairs,
or even three; once I was foolish enough to see such vain
little reactions as acts of courage, but I have outgrown them
now, they cost me too dearly, the useless chairs hindered my
movements, weighed heavy on my arms, beat against my

legs, worst of all I was only abetting my enemies by con-
forming to their idea of me, apparently acknowledging the
unnatural, outrageous, and perfectly gratuitous nature of
my practices when I should have turned away from my de-
tractors and worked toward acceptance from my fellows,
gradually, without effrontery, through the simple openness
of my character and the modesty of my words, and with
just the one chair on my head. This was the course I even-
tually chose to follow, and I still stick to it today, despite the
snickers and whispers I hear as I pass by, most commonly
emanating from sad characters racked by bitterness and
self-loathing, who hope to leave the losers behind and take
the side of the masters by fixing their hatred upon me: why
should I care if some pig-eyed social climber tries to push
me into the muck with his snout? But alas, the most worthy
and respectable folk are just as stupefied by the sight of me,
half perplexed, half amused, Méline was the first to take the
thing in without indignation or laughter. People clearly do
not understand that however unusual I may be, I am nonetheless unexceptional and that this chair over which they
make such a fuss, this chair that undeservedly sets me apart
from the rest and condemns me to such a cruel kind of iso-
lation, this chair alone offers me a place in the community
– where would I be without it?

(Only once did I abandon my self-imposed restraint:
pursued by a large horde of horsemen dressed in tight, red

velvet jackets – we offered the birds the spectacle of a chair fleeing a pack of theater seats – terrified by the braying of their horns and the baying of their hounds, soon cornered in a ravine with the barrel of every rifle trained on me, I turned to face the enemy, head down, I charged, I sent a few dogs flying, I eviscerated a few horses, and the hunters' beautiful fitted jackets ended up with a few rips and punctures . . . but that time my life was at stake.)

I offered to let Kolski have my room. He chose to come with me. As if sensing my reluctance, he volunteered to carry the chairs to the work site himself, four at a time, two under each arm. Many were the timid young brides in their wedding dresses who appeared at their windows to watch him pass by, or so at least he chose to see the suspicious widows draped in tulle curtains, warily observing his movements from behind their parlor windows, and surely he did them no harm by seeing them as such: in Kolski's poetic system, it is by fully trusting in appearances that one begins to reshape the world. In fact, he took such pleasure in moving our belongings that afterward he often came to me and borrowed four chairs before going out for a walk. I'm not one of those people who can fit onto just one chair, he explained to me, I'm not one of those meek thinkers who keeps all his ideas in just one head, and whose pinched little buttocks are just as unlikely to spill over the edges of their allotted nine hundred square centimeters of straw, I would never voluntarily reduce myself to myself like that, and besides, what puny body sitting there motionless like that could ever be enough for me? Instead of hunching over my own bones as if I were going to gnaw on them – which is what you expect from a person in a chair, to eat himself and disappear – and limiting my thoughts only to what can be absorbed by the sponge that is my brain, I find it more fitting to walk with your chairs surrounding me, their unwieldy weight heightening my discomfort, aggravating my fatigue: it becomes a pleasure to refuse their wheedling invitation, to pervert them, to corrupt those chairs, ever faithful to their race and to their masters, so thoroughly convinced we are human that it becomes impossible to doubt it, by using them in a way perfectly contrary to their intended purpose, dragging them along like a heavy burden, ill-bound faggots beneath that wholesome veneer. But make no mistake, I share your admiration for furniture makers, for the men who hew and saw the wood, who turn and shape it to create regular geometric forms that can be easily stowed away against walls or in corners, ridding the forest glades of fallen trees so that we might sit on the stumps and eat our lunch.

*

We now live in two adjoining bungalows whose common interior door, standing open on our arrival, has not been shut since. Kolski doesn't like doors either, insurmountable barriers, as he says, to those less solidly wooden than they: discretion and modesty are useless if we can't even enter a room without displacing hundreds of cubic meters of air, more than the wing of a stork flying from Alsace to the Cape of Good Hope; as we push open the door so we can go and waste some time in the next room, we resemble nothing so much as the card player who with a powerful haymaker lays out on the green felt tabletop not the winning card his mighty gesture foretold, the one that would have scooped up and carried off the chips, but instead some hapless jack of clubs, an eternal loser, sprawled out together with his pitiful double in the glare of the overhead lights – they're carried off together, head to toe, on the same stretcher. As an alternative to the door, Kolski proposes a system modeled on the matchbox, by which structures would be built with drawers, each room of the house or apartment sliding in or out, independently of the rest, along rails concealed in the building's frame. A room could be opened to the sky halfway or completely by remote control, or closed up and cast into complete darkness, hermetically sealed, without that ray of light under the door forming the line of the horizon (which, as it happens, is where enemies always come from, the hordes of Huns led by my mother, time to get up and go to school, surely you remember those barbarians who drank toasts from their victims' skulls).

*

It wasn't long after we moved in that I met Méline, as reported above, and undertook to educate her, by example at first, never allowing her to see me without a chair on my head, not even when our relationship, growing closer from day to day, became dangerous for her as well as me, since we could scarcely stir anymore without kneeing or elbowing each other and soon found ourselves forced to move in a single rhythm, lips pressed together. And in this way Méline learned that my chair, far from hampering my mobility, added a pleasurable sort of complication to our little games, inflamed the imagination of our interlaced bodies, allowed a thousand novel positions: we were innovators in a field whose most recent developments dated back to the distant India of the fourth century.

Méline accepted my gift, a pinewood chair, very light, very elegant, she promised to practice wearing it. Several times already we've ventured into the city streets this way, oblivious to jeers – their venom is diluted in our veins: two bodies become one, that's too much blood for the asp, it drowns.

("What if I asked you to put down your chair to prove your love, would you obey me?" In response to Méline's question, I picked up a rusty shovel blade from among the work site debris, brought it down with great force on my bare right foot, then wrapped the five severed toes in a handkerchief and pressed the bloody bundle into her hand: "No.")

One day she'll understand. She'll wonder how she ever did without her chair. We will raise our children in accordance with the tenets of our beliefs (I've seen some very nice little chairs made of plastic or wicker in the shops). Then evolution will take over for us: however reluctant she might be at first, Nature always relents in the end and orders the morphological changes required whenever the body, by constraint or by choice, takes up new habits, new stances more favorable to its development; after a few generations the skeleton incorporates the corresponding modifications, slight adjustments or more radical structural reforms, we all remember how prehistoric man came to stand erect as his hands, freshly uprooted, his fingernails still encrusted with dirt, grew in agility. The body produces the proper amounts of all the necessary substances, thus connective tissue, the forerunner of bone, already contains the elastic protein (elastin) from which I expect great things, for I foresee the day when the 208 elements of the human skeleton will be augmented by the twelve interlocking pieces that form a chair, there's nothing standing in the way; the trapezoidal seat, melded with the parietal and frontal bones, will take its place in the family of flat bones that make up the skull, the legs in front and the backrest supports behind will be classified as long bones, beside the femurs and humeri, the crosspieces of the backrest, like the other vertebrae, among the short bones, and this new framework will be covered over by our tender flesh, furnishing etiquette books with a new bone of contention, opposing the partisans and the foes of nudity – should we reserve for the lover alone the right to see and touch these delicate members, or shall we flaunt them shamelessly before the world? – but there will be plenty of time to decide these questions and others of equal importance once the mutation has finally taken place.

 ✳

In the meantime, Méline refuses to move in with me, cites mysterious reasons, claims that the work site is about to be bulldozed, she saw it in the papers, they're going to put up a replica of a traditional African village, with families of black actors living in mud huts and staging scenes from the daily life of bush-dwellers for school groups and ethnology fans – ritual dances, outdoor cooking, wood and leather crafts – in the unspoken hope that they will lose themselves in their roles and rediscover, buried deep in their genetic memory, the ways and customs of their ancestors and through these social atavisms lend the enterprise an authoritative credibility, allowing visitors to observe those people's quaint ways without simulacrum, in real time and life size, and to experience the delicious fear that they might end up roasted and eaten, but also, why not, by special governmental authorization, to capture a vigorous young man or a girl of twelve and sell them into slavery.

Finally, after a few years, they plan to educate the savages, to teach them an intelligible language, the rudiments of basic culture and political theory, the one true religion, all our technological know-how, they have so much to learn, and how they will chuckle at their former backwardness as they screw our little strangled suns into the ceiling above their heads! (Behold as I lay bare for you the many mysteries of this attic, cries the angel of electric light, a dusty deathtrap full of worthless junk, yesterday's antiques, caved-in suitcases stuffed with old rags and yellowed papers: one bulb at the end of a wire and all is revealed.) In fact, two or three such villages can already be found in the countryside of our beautiful land, but this one will have an added attraction, a zoological park to be built next door at the same time, housing fauna from the African ecosystem, with a communicating gateway that will permit the inhabitants of the village to hunt in the park, and vice versa, after hours – and on each side, the losses will be counterbalanced by the births.

So, says Méline, it would be wrong to upset the tranquillity of her family's existence and leave the huge apartment where they have always lived only to share my bungalow for a few weeks before being tossed into the street with no possibility, however remote, of returning to her childhood bedroom, by then undoubtedly rented out to a student on whom her parents would bestow all their frustrated affections and dreams; she can easily picture that tall, thin, bespectacled orphan girl, self-serving and studious, tireless in her efforts to gain their favor and replace the runaway in their hearts, even if it means simulating filial sentiments and using elaborate tricks of makeup or hairstyling to underscore some vague points of physical resemblance she thinks she might share with one or the other of them, or perhaps both: sharpening her long nose with a knife to give it an edge like her landlady's, Méline's mother, and eternally squinting behind her glasses in an attempt to touch the heart of Méline's extremely nearsighted father, two burdens that their genuine daughter fortunately did not inherit, since Méline's nose and eyes are such that you would swear you were looking at an ocellated butterfly, perching on a rosebud. In vain I try to reassure her, I explain that she will never find herself out on the street, that no one and nothing could force her out of her chic, cozy, white beechwood parlor, that she can easily lock herself inside if she wants to – how? With a single gesture I rotate the chair on my head, my hands clutch at the uprights of the backrest, and I smile at her through the shelter of the bars. But Méline will not give in. She doesn't want to let some strange woman usurp the place she occupies in her parents' hearts, down at the end of the hall, a sunny room with a private bath and two tall windows overlooking the street, and besides that, my lovely white chair flattens her hairdo.

*

I do have one follower, however, to whom such concerns mean nothing, a new arrival at the work site, not particularly appealing at first sight, Egger: a long, yellow face, thin lips, two ocular globes visible almost in their entirety, slipping free of the limp grasp of his eyelids, but that could no less easily flow from his gaping nostrils and slowly disappear into the dense network of wrinkles covering his blood-clotted face (or is that thick wine aging in his veins?), while his receding lower jaw sets off the deep, dark hole that is his mouth, just as, up above his straight nose, shapely but slightly off course, indeed grotesquely twisted, his huge forehead, smoother and more convex than a cheek of the man in the Moon, suddenly creases and shrinks until it disappears into the undergrowth of the eyebrows, through which his eyes shine like two moist smiles through a beard, and, similarly, his entire body first swells then collapses, like octopus flesh, his arms and legs extend and retract – Egger is racked by constant nervous tics, which also affect his voice and the waves in his hair, now frizzy, now lank, such that we cannot designate as his any one face from among those he displays within a few seconds, now you see him, now you don't, a whole crowd jostling each other beneath his clothes, all trying to thrust a head out the neck hole of his shirt in a desperate plea for attention, my attention as it happens, since they latched on to me the moment they saw me, as one man, Egger and company, now jammed together beneath a single kitchen chair borrowed from Madame Stempf, fighting for the right to express their admiration for me:

"Because you're right! You are the first to understand that it is madness to go on living without a chair upside down on your head. Why has no one seen this until now? How is it possible that even today so few follow your example, that so few see the obvious superiority of this evolutionary step, this promise of new pleasures and joys, this revolution without tears, so effortlessly carried off? That one simple act of putting a chair on your head – let all mankind follow your lead, and the world will be transformed for the greater good of us all, without bloodshed, with no heroic struggles to drain the reformer's energy. You alone have realized that we can no longer hope to weaken the underpinnings of a civilization sunk deep into its own filth, or to rock its foundations, long since fused with the Earth's crust through fossilization – even the deepest geological strata hold less natural sediment than old coins and rubble from temples and prisons. Our only chance is to make our stand, as you have done, in the virgin space above our heads, high in the heavens but within our reach. You can count on my complete devotion."

An unambiguous profession of faith, then, repeated and expanded upon in turns by an old and withered Egger, his sunken cheeks bathed in shadows, then by a vigorous Egger who beats his breast or slaps himself roughly on the back as he speaks, by a heavy-lidded Egger who sniffles mightily while slowly shaking his head, by a sweaty Egger, bloated, grumpy, with upturned mustachioes, by a stuttering Egger, young again, who stands on tiptoe and spins in circles like a child, by other Eggers, even more ephemeral, less powerfully portrayed, just as full of conviction, keeping up the patter, adding their bit without missing a beat from under the kitchen chair, a crowd of supporters of all ages assuring me one after another of their complete devotion.

A man had four sons and little wealth. As he grew older he began to neglect his business, then he fell ill; he was forced to sell his lands to pay for his doctors and his medicine. He would die with nothing left to pass on to his sons, and that knowledge darkened his final days. Let my experience in life at least be of some use to my children, he said to himself, and he resolved to give them each a precious piece of advice as their inheritance, thanks to which they would make their fortune and find happiness on Earth. And so the dying man called his sons to his bedside and ordered them to go forth at once, each following a separate path, toward the four points of the compass, and to bring back the first thing that caught their eye when they were five hundred paces from home. For Fortune always smiles on those who know how to exploit her, and I will show you how to profit from your discovery. The sons did as their father wished. On their return, he called them together once again around his deathbed.

"My son," he said to the eldest, who held an apple in his hand, "eat that apple, it will make a good meal, and then you must gather up the seeds and plant them, they will grow into beautiful trees that will give you all the food you need, and you will plant their seeds and sell the rest of the fruit in the market. Thus your happiness and your fortune on this Earth are assured. This lifts a heavy burden from my heart."

He then named the younger brother, who stepped forward and showed his father a book.

"My son," he told him, "read that book, it will help you to pass the time pleasantly and to increase your knowledge. Then you must teach others what it has taught you, and then, with the money your students give you, buy other books, read them all, increase your knowledge, and your students will grow ever more numerous. Thus your happiness and your fortune on this Earth are assured. This is a sweet consolation to me."

Then he called the third son, who raised a tangled piece of string before his father's eyes.

"My son," he told him, "untangle that string, unwind it, weight it on one end with a small stone. You will then have a plumb line with which you will erect sound, solid walls, and your reputation as an architect will soon be established. Thus your happiness and your fortune on this Earth are assured. This is a great comfort to me."

Finally he turned to the fourth son, who was holding a dead penguin by one wing.

"My son," he said to him, "will you let go of me!" shrieked Madame Stempf, applying a full-body slam to the two policemen trying to pull her to her feet, "I forbid you to raise a hand against my children!" Hearing these words, one of the thugs burst into her trailer, expecting to find cowering in terror the brats whose existence she had so carelessly given away – "Where have you hidden your kids?" he asked as he came out again, while she protected her belly with her outstretched arms and, with a menacing gaze, kept the other brute at bay, forcing him to vent his wrath on the bundled rushes stacked up nearby, trying to break them over his knee, showing his ignorance of the flexibility of rushes; the bundle bent but didn't break, and, like a stouthearted wrestler pinned to the mat who at the last possible moment bursts into action and overturns his foe, it snapped back, whipping the fat policeman in the face, and he, receiving all at once the hundred lashes he so richly deserved, fell backward onto his fellow policeman, equally fat, who tottered and collapsed in his turn. As we know, this sort of breakneck silent scene is traditionally followed by the arrival of sound: "You have five minutes to pack your things and get the hell out of here!"

*

Let me make this quite clear: I am not prone to delusions of persecution, I suspect that sparrows were not put on Earth to spy on me, that the Sun is not a spotlight aimed at my person, that the tiger is hungry for some reason other than because he is thinking about me; my suffering stems rather from nature's indifference to me, and from the countless things that never take my extended hand, but I can't escape the impression that if one looks past all the age-old conflicts besetting human relations, one will find one point of agreement, an absolute unanimity of the sort so rarely seen in this world, concerning me, against me, unspoken and unwritten, to wit, that every man has a duty to do his utmost to spoil my tranquillity, the only dream shared by all mankind, spoil my tranquillity, one common goal allowing the reconciliation of all the peoples of the globe, of the two sexes, of the generations, an irresistible imperative, a single law, never opposed, never doubted, as if this were indeed the necessary condition for any kind of progress, priority one: spoil my tranquillity, a project that has never lacked for volunteers, many and zealous, giving freely of their time, throwing themselves body and soul into their work, wholeheartedly, and I must say success-fully, with a tenacity that never flags, on the contrary, since now the forces of public order have become involved, as if their mission to keep the peace required them first and foremost to spoil my tranquillity, as if the world would never sleep peacefully so long as I, myself, enjoyed a taste of tranquillity. It's not as if I don't closet myself away in order to find it, I hole up, it's not as if I make a display of myself when I happen upon it, I become in fact the small-est of men, nearly invisible, the most unremarkable of all despite my chair, which is not in and of itself a sign of my tranquillity, which furthermore I also wear when things are going badly, but my discretion does not protect me (for I would find this collective obsession with spoiling my tranquillity much easier to understand if I paraded it immodestly amid tumult and panic), it makes no difference, my tranquillity is deemed unacceptable, intolerable, it does irreparable harm to I know not what, it is vital that it be stopped without delay, for that they give their all, every force is mobilized, even the most minor – if I were on a desert island, off in mid-ocean, some lumberjack would row ashore and cut down my palm tree to deprive me of shade, then head back to his boat, turning around one last time to spit into my water source or slash the teat of my goat – no sooner have I found a home somewhere, no sooner have I dug my hole, than along comes some disruption to make my life unlivable and send me on my way.

*

And so they came, a whole troop of them, a squadron, a brigade, a squad, first thing in the morning, Méline was right, a thousand fat policemen came to send us packing, and how were we to stop them? I was still asleep when they stormed the work site, crashing through our fragile rampart of corrugated tin and erupting into our trailers as indelicately as you please, they even ripped Malton and Lanson's door from its hinges. I suppose they were hoping to arouse some sort of resistance so that they could then crush us without remorse – the one they call Malton charged toward our men on his rolling machine, they managed, barely, to take shelter behind a wall of fire propped up with hand grenades – but we refused to play the game, except Topouria: finding a certain family resemblance between the crane and the war machines of antiquity, the ballista or the catapult for instance, he grasped a concrete pillar between his arms and tried to uproot it, intending to spin it rapidly above his head and launch it against the enemy, decimating their ranks and forcing them to beat a hasty retreat carrying their dead and wounded; but his efforts failed, as the enemy saw it, he was merely trying to hold fast to his position, they forced him to disengage by means of raps on the knuckles. At the same time, Kolski suddenly threw open all the wooden crates in which he was keeping his supply of darkness, collected and boxed up one moonless night – a stockpile accumulated in preparation for a series of ambitious experiments aimed at the development of a machine to produce shadow, no more difficult to operate than a lamp, which would allow the user to create complete darkness without turning out the lights or closing the shutters, negative actions, nihilistic even, thanks to which the confusion of Evil with darkness remains with us, stronger than ever, whereas the lucid, joyous, fecund gesture of switching on his diffuser will disperse that swarm of devils and witches, left over from outmoded mythologies, night will once again bring us hope and confidence in the days to come. But Kolski's hoard of darkness was not enough to cover the work site, the early morning light was veiled only a little at ground level, thickened, a slightly murky fog enveloped the pile of sand atop which the chief of the brigade had perched to oversee the operations, providing, unbeknownst to himself, a simple explanation for the stationary flight of archangels, for so he seemed, standing on a cloud and exerting his will with finger and eye: we soon found ourselves on the pavement.

*

Violently shoved from behind, Malton was the first one through the broken palisade, roughly pushed along, his wheelchair, thrown off balance, rolled along on the two right-hand wheels for a moment, then crashed back to earth, Lanson caught up with him and managed to stop it before the slope carried him down to the river. Kolski and Topouria followed, the one landing on the other without serious injury; then it was Madame Stempf's turn, hands on her stomach, dragging her feet, in the arms of two policemen who, once outside, on the other side of the fence, let her drop to the ground and slump backwards, one foot folded beneath her body. I had tried – without success, excepting those we had put on for the night – to save a few chairs with Egger's help, and we were the last to be expelled, flung to the sidewalk with the rest. Egger was pleased, I think, to be treated just as I was. He has dogged my steps from the moment he set foot here. His very size and position, beside me or in front of me (because he does sometimes precede me when my destination is not in doubt), or behind me, on my heels, seem to change according to the time of day, perhaps depending on the height of the Sun in the sky: Egger revolves around me like a shadow that grows or shrinks, blazes the trail or brings up the rear, but sticks close by and never has to be called to heel; he repeats my every gesture after a brief, almost imperceptible lag, my every footstep is doubled. At noon, our blood merges. I think I could suddenly cast myself headlong or spring backward and never surprise or dishearten him. I also sometimes think he would follow me just the same, without a moment's hesitation, and recreate my movements no less faithfully if I suddenly set my chair on the ground and sat down upon it, that he had put a chair on his head not because he'd suddenly grasped the advantages of my way of life, nor because my edifying example had opened his eyes, but because a man of his sort, uncertain, unstable, needs to impose some sort of discipline on himself to keep from losing his way and disappearing into the crowd of his fleeting incarnations, and so does not hesitate to take on someone else's personality, having no particular personality of his own, some more solidly and harmoniously structured personality, and not an ordinary one, devoid of eminence and so exerting no influence on him – he would rather entrust the conduct of his life to someone whose superiority over him seems beyond doubt, who can impress him sufficiently to justify his complete submission. In sum, Egger was looking for a master, any master, or, more precisely, a model, and nothing else mattered to him: my one disciple would just as happily have become the disciple of a bear trainer or a Catholic astrophysicist if one or the other of them, rather than me, had crossed his path. Can I honestly believe, then, that I have won him over to my cause? I would rather see the bear trainer or the Catholic astrophysicist abandon their meaningless endeavors to follow my lead, struck by the obvious truth, enlightened, I would rather see the king crown himself with his overturned chamber pot; then I could truly say that my policies had triumphed.

But is it not blindingly clear that, for the moment, Egger is my only active partisan, notwithstanding Kolski's support and Méline's and others' benevolence, the first to follow so precisely in my footsteps? And is it my place to judge his reasons for doing so? Indeed, is there a wrong reason for wearing a chair upside down on your head? His are surely no less valid than mine.

We watched the bulldozers advance. They passed before us as we lay prostrate – even Topouria was still, the weak rumble of a dying motor made his lip tremble just a little, nothing more – and entered the work site in single file. The demolition was underway. Our trailers were first on the list for destruction, I gathered, and my chairs were undoubtedly broken, shattered, their slender legs crushed beneath the blades of those stupid machines conceived to satisfy man's basest instincts, the brutal desires his powerless body must repress. But I didn't stick around to watch the pillage. The policemen, standing in closed ranks before the palisade, threatened to take us downtown if we didn't disappear *(sic)*. Méline won't mind putting us up for a while, I thought.

There's no denying that the Raffins' apartment is huge, since Méline's father is employed by a vast commercial enterprise to perform one of those incomprehensibly lucrative jobs that consists of wiggling the fingertips to create ephemeral columns of names and numbers on a computer screen, all the while conversing on the telephone with an American who never fails to screw you royally; nevertheless it lacks the floor space for seven visitors in addition to its four inhabitants, Monsieur and Madame Raffin, Méline, and her younger brother, Hans: each has a private bedroom, then there's a living-dining room, a library-study – do not make the mistake of inferring from these hyphenated spaces that the Raffin family lives in quarters so cramped that they have to put the merest broom closet to multiple uses, quite the contrary; the difficulty is that it seems impossible to occupy rooms this voluminous without inventing arbitrary divisions and so formulating a number of different reasons to be there at various times of day, unless, presumably, you are a javelin thrower working from home, odd idea, in which case the main room would of course be entirely and indivisibly reserved for that purpose, but then where are you to store your javelins after the workout if not in the broom closet, which is too large for brooms alone anyway – who keeps twelve brooms in the house at once? – which is also where the Raffins store their supply of umbrellas and tennis rackets, just as the giant shoe closet in the front hallway houses an impressive collection of economics periodicals, along with countless pairs of shoes, secured on coat hooks or stacked on shelves – it would seem that every step taken by the Raffin family leads inexorably to this cubbyhole, their gambols in flip-flops along dusty footpaths no less than their strolls through city streets, every sidestep and detour they're forced to make by snow, rain, mud, freshly waxed floors, schoolyards, and sports fields, while far above their clumsy clomping, Méline's ballerina slippers, suspended from a rod, perform *entrechats* in the dark – and there is yet another bedroom tucked away in the apartment, furnished for their houseguests' convenience with an ancient fold-out couch that can not only be made to adopt a sitting or prone position but also, through the play of concealed springs, sometimes rolls into a ball or stands erect; then there's a storage room and closet where Madame Raffin's ghostly furs, on their wooden hangers, recall another sort of stuffed mammal, those of which a paw rests gently on a varnished branch. Every bedroom is equipped with running water and its inevitable hanger-on (on the wall, a mirror), thereby realizing the first condition necessary to the age-old dream of autarky, and there is no doubt that we would soon see a separatist movement arise and flourish behind every barricaded door were it not for the shared bathroom and its irresistible attractions, the deep blue waves of its bathtub, the life-giving rain of its shower, and the kitchen, an idyllic spot lined with green ceramic, defended by pots of boiling oil and a whole arsenal of cutlery, communi-cating only with the dining room and only at mealtimes, which leaves the family no choice but to unite twice a day, Louis-René Raffin, Clotilde Raffin, Méline Raffin, Hans Raffin, meeting at a table beneath which Woff, the animal of the house, neither a cat nor a goldfish, waits for the breadcrumbs, scraps of ham, and cheese rinds – he's not a young calf either – that enliven his ordinary diet, and yes you have to take him outside every morning and evening, but, on the other hand, the trash can only has to be taken out twice a week, a tradeoff made all the more attractive by the fact that Woff is a male, full of beans, whose outpourings bring in a tidy sum, he sleeps on a cushion in the living room – nor a horse.

*

A huge apartment, then, but there were seven of us, and Méline, fearing her father's reaction, ushered us hastily into her room, where it was immediately clear that we couldn't move a little finger without causing an uncontainable ripple effect, the waves coming closer and closer together, reinforcing each other as dictated by the savage logic of repercussion, such that the last body to be affected by that tiny gesture's accumulated force reeled as if in the throes of violent paroxysms, becoming in its turn the source of the most devastating perturbations. Tossed by this chaotic ebb and flow, Malton's wheelchair tipped over backward and rolled the length of the wall until at last it struck the ceiling, where it righted itself again, with Lanson in hot pursuit, his fists still clenched around the handles, and Egger following in his footsteps. Next Topouria, his body stiff, his arms outstretched, clasped his hands around Madame Stempf's hips, and, using her as a counterweight, performed an aerial half rotation that propelled him into their midst. I helped him hoist the caner up, then, with Kolski by my side, under our own steam, climbed up to join them, and all the while Méline stood by, reluctant to follow us.

✶

Already we could see more clearly. Already we could breathe more easily. The surface area we had at our disposal on the ceiling was of course the same as that of the bedroom below but uncluttered by all that furniture: Méline's bed and nightstand, a small desk, an upright piano and its indispensable rotating stool, wound up as high as it will go, the secret key to the mechanism that moves the pianist's fingers, it's high time that was known, two bookshelves, laden with books and various objects of sentimental value (the most delicate sentiments inevitably crystallize around horrid, gaudy, multicolored gewgaws, or pathetic cracked things), and finally the armoire, where a thousand girlish costumes are hung or stacked, sporty, sophisticated, summery, shivery, along with a panoply of other disguises that fool no one: there's no mistaking it, that's Méline rippling beneath them, it's obvious, even blinded by two or three thicknesses of wool or cotton, my index finger can easily locate the little dark spot northeast of her navel.

On the ceiling we had elbow room, somewhat limited perhaps, but at least we could take a step or two without crashing into each other. A pure white surface, unsullied as snow still in the cloud, without the slightest asperity, neither hole nor bump, perfectly flat, easy on the feet, a joy to walk on: Kolski was the first – soon seconded by Egger – to take off his shoes, useless prostheses to him now, they fell vertically, blazing a trail for the rest – not even Malton wanted to keep his on – fourteen shoes in all, which Méline pushed under her bed, where they met up with a fifteenth, a black pump lost twelve years earlier by a clumsy doll who has since become a svelte, willowy mannequin in the window of a lingerie shop, assuming, that is, that she grew like her little playmate did, having had the same education and shared all her meals.

*

Despite our newfound contentment, and the sense of perfect serenity after the morning's painful events, my joy was not unmixed. I felt profoundly uncomfortable, in fact, a sensation all the more unexpected because it was caused by my chair. This chair, to which I had grown so intimately attached, my sole defense, my one support, the very foundation of my being, for the first time in my life my chair had become a nuisance: its feet knocked against the furniture in the room, a bookshelf tottered, several times I had to crouch down on the ceiling to avoid wounding Méline below me. Worse yet, and difficult to imagine, I could feel my chair weighing me down! In this new situation, my chair was not only a bother, not only a danger, but a burden! Never before had I known it to produce any effect but lightness, or, more precisely, elevation. It lifted me higher. My place was laid and waiting at the heavenly table. I fairly flew. And now that same chair had become a yoke, and I the ox that it bent toward the ground. It's a very heavy thing, a chair is, once it has ceased to support you. But I couldn't simply drop it, simply and suddenly bisect myself by tearing off a piece of me that might well be worth more than the other, toward which, in any case, all eyes, all thoughts and comments are unfailingly directed from the first glance onward, oblivious to all aspects of my person contained between the soles of my feet and the summit of my skull. (Méline's eye is equally blind to me, too piercing, for her alone that bright little beam projects a girlish dream of which I am the starry-eyed hero – the same sunbeam illuminates a shard of glass deep in the muddy river,

and the girl honestly believes that this unreal, pale glimmer
is the color of the water, and that my eyes are green – her
hand brushes against my sallow, blank, plump face, alien
to everyone but me, and Méline smiles at the flawless
reflection of her smile in my ugly teeth; sometimes even a
string of nacre pearls on her neck doubles and widens that
marvelous smile – what did I do to deserve that? where does
she come up with these things?)

      *

One thing was sure, however, one fact beyond dispute: it
was my chair that had brought me here. Before the salad
days in the warehouse, back when, unable to pay the rent on
my room, I used to spend most of my time outside so I
wouldn't be tossed out into the street, the cold often drove
me to seek some sort of shelter; even then, no sooner had I
found my way into some apartment or small house than my
chair offered me a place on the ceiling, its four legs gently
coming to rest against it, surefooted, without a wobble, it
held fast, solidly braced, and immediately I felt much more
at peace than I did back in my room, tucked away beneath
my apartment building's mansard roof (which takes its
name from the architect François Mansart, a dreamer, an
incompetent sea captain, capsized keel topmost, a digger of
aerial graves for birds and angels), here I had a sense of per-
manence, of being beyond the reach of rent collectors, poor

down-to-earth souls, no spring in their step. I was on virgin territory here, untended, you could see from a single glance that it wasn't inhabited, had never been inhabited, and there was no reason to believe it ever would be, no trace of construction in progress, I was usurping no one's place by settling there, neither ousting nor disturbing a soul. I was a pioneer, and, as such, owner and master of the place, free to furnish it as I liked. No one could have accused me of flaunting an opulent lifestyle before those who lived below me, who lived down in the room I quickly passed through, and often on tiptoe, in order to set my chair on the ceiling, my one piece of furniture, the central, single object in my little sitting room – and I would certainly have taken up residence there for good, except that my feet were still touching the floor, meaning that even if I stood perfectly still, I nevertheless inconvenienced the owners and masters of the carpet. Furthermore, they were inevitably unhappy to find me there, when, after a day taken up with work and errands – a series of brief emergences of the sort turtles make – they dragged their aching heads and broken limbs back inside, only to find me standing there; they never welcomed me with open arms. However greatly I delighted in finding myself on the ceiling and out of reach, I suffered in equal measure from this constant exposure to insults, threats, and sometimes blows from the people living below me. This mingling of

contradictory sensations soon made the situation intolerable. The right hand, as it caresses a breast, cannot entirely
ignore the dog gnawing on the left. I went on my way.

Outside stood the city's denuded trees; I was one of
them, without visible roots, not so much planted in the
soil as hanging there, clutching at the sky with our few
bare branches, indeed I was the most luxuriant of them all,
thanks to the garlands and acanthus leaves strewn about
my upper story; for the city fathers, yearning to be immor-
talized in sculpture, have the trees trimmed in their image
– how else to explain this procession of misshapen trunks
and stunted limbs?

But I was soon drawn back inside. The cold was only an
excuse. The dwellings of my fellow men were calling me,
despite the inconvenience and the hostile reception I knew
I'd find there, for never once was I invited in, and if I was
foolish enough to announce my presence by ringing the
bell, they quickly bolted the door: I heard the key turning
in the lock, twice, thrice, like an idiotic little ballerina on a
music box, I'd shot myself in the foot, and I was left hop-
ping about in place until exhaustion overcame me. Despite all this, then, I came back inside, I entered apartments by force, breaking a window, I'm hardheaded. I had
a look around. I didn't know what I was doing there, nor
why I'd been so desperate to see these interiors, where everything seemed alien and incomprehensible to me. Nev-

ertheless, the layout of the place, always more or less the same, suggested that family life was ordered by a system both universally accepted and unfailingly reproduced, the narrow alleyways winding through the furniture always led to the same preordained locales, each reserved for one or two specific activities, themselves thoroughly regimented (love in the kitchen in no way escaping the rule) and allowed no behavior outside those principles. There's no way out of it, except perhaps throwing yourself from a window, and even then, is that deadly vertical drop not precisely the fate designed for dissidents, the outcome planned for them from the moment of the system's conception, taking them permanently out of the picture before they can become dangerous? Even then I thought of settling on the ceiling and never leaving it again. I have already described the welcome that awaited me when the returning inhabitants caught sight of me, my flanks still bear the traces of blows inflicted with broom or fireplace poker (an old lady), which taught me nothing, no more than the terror I felt in those stifling, cramped spaces, since as soon as I found myself outside, I've already said this as well, my only thought was to return. It was strange; I didn't want to go back, everything in me found it repugnant, my legs themselves refused to carry me, wormed their way out of the task, not cravenly but craftily, using alibis – my right foot was learning to paint and couldn't bear to put down the brush, for instance – and yet on I went, at full speed, back to the dreaded apartments, and it was my chair that led me there. My quadrupedal chair, breaking into a three-step midair gallop, charging wildly, had ceased to obey my commands, I followed its movements like a rider ensnared in the tail of his horse. For the chair is built for speed, see in this same vein the leopard, justly famous for its bursts of kinetic energy, with its flat back, its four long, slender legs, its elegantly trim lines, equally capable of sitting impassive and still for great lengths of time before exploding into a sprint, there's more than one similarity between the two, a disturbing twinlike quality, and indeed the sumptuous tastes of the Roman patrician, craving symmetry in all things, found nothing so attractive as a chair and a leopard in the atrium. You probably have no idea how fast a chair is, you who pin it to the ground with all your weight, sometimes it gives way under you, you roll in the dust, dismayed, abraded, serves you right – must I repeat once again that it is a serious misuse of a chair to treat it as a seat? So many men have sat on chairs before us, to take their place is inevitably to share their plate. I have no appetite for that regurgitated ragout. My upturned chair has allowed me to soar high above the common vicissitudes of existence, for which it constituted a serious handicap, a pair of wings on my back would not have done the job as well, and would have made of me an oversized and rather ridiculous turkey. In the end, it brought me here, to Méline's, on the ceiling, with my friends. The time had come to part with it. Immediately imitated by Egger, then by Malton, who had finally found the freedom of movement stolen from him by paralysis down below, I dropped my chair.

The head you chop off does not stop thinking, in spite of it all, as with one blow of the blade, it is detached from the shoulders, it feels that migraine with perfect lucidity, it senses the weight, the cold, the shock of the metal as it splits the vertebrae, the sharpened steel plunging deep into the flesh, slicing it cleanly, conscious to the last, the severed head knows it's all over, as it falls, it understands that no fiber now connects it to the body, the torment is brief, but while it lasts, the train of thought accelerates, leaving me plenty of time to recall my entire life from the beginning, a fearful child seeking shelter in the hole and under the roof furnished by kyphosis, the procedure chosen for my treatment, the unforeseen well-being it granted me, simultaneously founding the great talent I would soon display in the exercise of my profession, my endless walks through the city in search of a brother or a kindred spirit, my stay in the refrigerated warehouse, and later my acquaintance with Kolski, Méline, and the rest, our move to the deserted library work site, the assault on our homes by the forces of order, our arrival at the Raffins', first heaped up in Méline's room, then blissful on the ceiling, the doubts that nevertheless overcame me there, and my decision to rid myself of them in the only way I could – finally my chair crashes to earth, shatters as it hits the floor, the crosspieces of the backrest snap, I couldn't care less, I no longer need that little ladder to rise above the turmoil.

Another necessary clarification: I have never thought myself an angel. That mistake was not mine. People looked me over from top to bottom, a powerful lever, sufficient in itself to hoist me from among the mob, to lift me unto the heavens. I never asked to be singled out this way. My chair gave me away as a troublemaker or a dangerous radical: a man who walked the streets with a chair on his head might just as well derail trains or explode planes; if he could take a piece of furniture designed for rest and pause on such interminably long walks, his perversion would surely lead him one day into an inverse desire to hamper the circulation of winged or wheeled vehicles, and even the natural movements of animate beings – I became an assassin, and of the worst kind, one who hasn't yet committed his crime. Here was the source of the misunderstanding: they interpreted my way with a chair as an attempt to overturn established values and authorities, when in fact I always believed, quite to the contrary, that I was reestablishing the natural equilibrium by acting as I did, that I was setting things to rights, in addition to considerations of an aesthetic or hygienic nature, or of simple convenience, as well as my more personal reasons, having to do with my social ineptitude and my inability to find a place for myself in that sphere, which were, of course, not without a certain influence on my behavior.

I must also say that while I did sit on many occasions, it was always out of politeness to those who invited me to do so, first, and second, because I didn't dare contest the time-honored practices of those in my profession, who prefer to work seated, which proves my unilateral respect, by unilateral I mean not repaid, for the beliefs and customs of my contemporaries and forerunners, a respect all the more praiseworthy in that it forced me, for hours at a time, into positions that tested my sensitivities to the utmost – like the explorer compelled to share the rustic meal of his hosts, living snakes and dead enemies. Furthermore, while I never failed to enjoy the softness of a seat woven from marsh-growing reeds, it suddenly struck me how closely I resembled a man sunk up to the waist in that marsh, and my subsequent difficulties in extricating myself confirmed that first impression, which often proves to be a foretaste of the truth. I might add that the sensation of comfort can be perceived more fully and more subtly by my skull than by my butt, and more pleasurably as well, since the human skull is a rock-hard box of bone while the buttocks of the same beast, round, fleshy, soft, are such that any additional padding seems quite superfluous, and the act of slipping a seat beneath them akin to resting an armchair on an armchair.

*

The Raffins' apartment is ours, the entire surface of its ceiling, we would be fools not to put it to use. Méline opens the door of her room. This, as it happens, is the first real problem we must face, opening doors: from here it's impossible, the knob is too far away, we'll have to do something about that, either install a second knob linked to the other by a steel shaft, or else, more simply, raise the knob to make it accessible to us while still within reach from below. Topouria, who is not put off by small tasks requiring patience and precision, promises to take care of it, Egger too. On the other hand, we easily step over the block of wall that marks the threshold on our side of the door; Malton even hops playfully over it on his way out.

The hallway soothes our eyes after the disorientingly unfamiliar view in Méline's room, where our gaze drifted in bewilderment from the suspended furniture to the inverted pictures on the walls, this bare, empty space brings us back to a more traditional set of perspectives and angles, only the floral motif of the wallpaper disconcerts us a little – it takes a strange sense of interior decoration to adorn your walls with wilted bouquets falling through space, says Lanson, growing woozy.

This reverse vision of the world beneath us is rather disturbing, no point in denying it; Méline's face suddenly strikes me as unbearably ugly, according, at least, to the aesthetic criteria we have inherited from antiquity, to which I thought I was no longer subject: under a flabby little forehead, which forms a visor-like extension to a bald, repulsively flat skull, shaped like a clothes iron, the orbit of a single eye, recently gouged or punctured, reveals

16/8

between its swollen lids, tumefied and squinting, the bandage of pink flesh that blinds it; aging boxers, twenty bouts, twenty defeats, have a cleaner profile than hers, a nose like that could only grow under the hoof of a horse; two minuscule mouths suck at two black berries, glistening with saliva, rolling them around between discolored lips – not a single tooth to bite into them, but the gums are raw. Those twin leers, sprinkled with whiskers and, under the two lower lips, a thicker growth of peach-fuzz, overhang a chin in the shape of a slightly convex cliff, but smooth and featureless, to which clings a messy beard, rather like a voluminous shawl of tangled wool, whose only good point is that it partially hides the ingrown ears – you look hideous from this angle, says Méline.

*

It's a very worrying thing, these grim faces of ours, they pose a real threat to my relationship with Méline, and from a broader perspective they will not simplify our peaceful coexistence with those below. If we want to stand face to face as we used to, we will each have to throw our heads back, which means resigning ourselves to stiff necks as well as depriving ourselves of all contact with the inhabitants of our own surface, apart from the crashes and collisions that would inevitably ensue. Perhaps we could meet the gaze of those below by leaning over a mirror? They would do the same, and our eyes would lock via the play of interacting reflections. That's how visitors to the Scuola Grande di San Rocco in Venice view Tintoretto's Biblical scenes on the ceiling, never raising their eyes, carrying their mirrors slowly and carefully like overladen platters, and indeed sometimes a sudden, unexpected avalanche of little round loaves sends them tipping this way and that, although miraculously they always manage to contain it. But, in any case, we did not settle here so that we could better admire the nether world, and, if only Méline would consent to join us, I could easily do without seeing it at all, I know it well, I'll remember, I don't think it has anything more to teach me. But Méline leaves me again, summoned to lunch by her mother, she promises to bring us something to eat when she comes back.

We hadn't thought of that: how will we feed ourselves on the ceiling? For we will not always have Méline's help from below, nor do we wish to remain forever at the mercy of those on the floor. Let's take a tip from this fellow, suggests Egger, crouched over a long, gray spider – for the tubiteles, a denizen of the heights since time immemorial, solved the subsistence problem long ago – see it weave its web, the flies and moths it captures are also a delicacy for all our favorite birds, the quail, the partridge, the woodcock: why, then, should we wait for a bird to have previously digested them before we feed on those little bugs ourselves? We can set traps for them up here, they're the ceiling's native fauna, to the exclusion of all other animal populations, unless we believe, more correctly perhaps, that the category "insect" includes all those other populations, and so possesses its own wildcats, lambs, dogs, cows, crabs, stunted, minuscule, but displaying so perfectly and precisely the special features found among the large ones that the latter come to seem in comparison like giant inflated balloons, ham-handedly designed, only vaguely similar at best, and quite pointless in any case. Or else: there exists an insect that incarnates with impeccable accuracy each sentiment, each concept, each ambition, an insect that illustrates and delineates every personality, every behavior, every activity, an insect that gives flesh to each verb, and if the Earth had never been populated by anything other than insects, it would be just as it is now, but everything would be more delicate, finer, more precise. Egger goes on to remind us that insects are fully comestible, needing no preparation, raw, live, but as it happens we aren't hungry after all, despite the time, no longer a problem. Thus everything that seemed certain to make our life on the ceiling impossible turns out, now that we're here, to be perfectly innocuous; we've left those worries behind us, on the floor, they no longer trouble us: how will we bathe on the ceiling? Well yes, how will we bathe? But how would we become dirty?

*

From the hallway we can follow the conversation of the Raffins, clustered around the dining-room table. Hans is arguing with his father. Silence in counterpoint from the women. They all clink their dishes and silverware. Teenage rebellion has always found its fullest expression during family meals, set to the discreet music of forks, whose transcription for electric guitars is a serious mistake, says Kolski, that uselessly assimilates word and sound: the only effect of this tiresome redundancy is to raise the volume, so what? If you want to paint a poppy, for instance, the last color you should use, obviously, is red; any other color, properly understood, would work better. The flower's form, like the brushstrokes, will also depend on the color chosen, or vice versa, for a black poppy and a yellow poppy in no way resemble each other, despite their shared similarity to the poppies growing by the roadside, and, as for those who nevertheless . . . here Kolski breaks off to listen to another of Madame Stempf's stories, more interesting and quite germane, it was long ago – we're sitting in a circle around her, straining to hear over the Raffins' raised voices – two brothers shared the same passion for painting, but whereas the older one, tenderly loved and spoiled by their mother, was taught by the best masters in the best schools, the younger one, incessantly humiliated and beaten and then cast out of the paternal home – for the father shared the mother's feelings – was forced to hire himself out to building contractors as a menial painter. The older son found fame as a landscape artist, able to transpose a forest of oaks onto his canvas as if he were transplanting them into fertile soil, never stripping off a single leaf, and every one properly lobed, veined, nor a single acorn, and in the sky above a pale cloud lazily unraveling. Rich and revered, honored on all sides, he grew old without a second thought for his long-lost brother. One morning, before dawn, he set out for the countryside, planning to paint the sunrise, the precise instant when the sun arises and spreads its light over the land, still damp with dew. This would be his final work, after which he would set down his brushes and serenely wait for death to take him. He chose a broad meadow opening onto a vast horizon of trees and hills. As he was setting up his easel, he glimpsed, just ahead, amid the shadows of the waning night's final moments, the shape of a man, from behind, right arm raised, moving his hand as if to wave goodbye, and sometimes rising up on tiptoe as though he were trying to catch hold of something. When the first ray of light pierced the darkness, he hurriedly concealed his hand beneath his overcoat, but the old *paysagiste* could see that he was holding a paintbrush. The man's coat was spotted with paint, and there were large containers sitting open at his feet. No canvas, though, and no easel, but the sky was colored a fresh, gentle blue behind a gossamer veil formed by fine droplets of sunshine, and down in the grass, a tiny rainbow hopped on one leg, trying to extricate itself from a dew-pearled spiderweb stretched between three poppy stems. The air smelled of oil and turpentine. Suddenly relieved of the weight of a turtledove, a branch discreetly shook its foliage, a brief shower of green rain spattered the black dirt beneath the tree, and as the bird flew over the old painter, a white drop fell onto the collar of his smock. Finally the stranger turned around, the hair of his brush was still damp, dripping with the same mauve that covered the distant hills. The two brothers recognized each other, each stood staring silently at the other for many long minutes, then the older one fell to his knees in the grass, by now almost dry. Go on, you can sign it for me, I'm used to it, said his brother with a smile, disappearing into the landscape.

And as for those who paint a poppy red, Kolski resumed, they're too late anyway, the work has been done, it's like pummeling a clown's nose beneath your fists.

*

A door slams, Méline bursts furiously into the hallway, her face hardened by anger, rounder though, her hair shorter, and enraged as I've never seen her before, her legs and arms bare, thin, sinewy, covered with hair, it's Hans, her younger brother, who raises his eyes to the ceiling, sees us, and comes right up, behind him we hear shouting and stomping, hurried, coming closer, the door is violently thrown

open, now Méline bursts into the hallway, her face dis-
figured by anger, you can scarcely make out the gentle curve
of her nose, straddled by the tortoise-shell glasses that im-
prove her vision and exacerbate her eczema, with a soiled
napkin hanging parallel to her polka-dot necktie or vice
versa (they've been eating eggs, unless the dots are spots
and the spots dots, in which case it was tomatoes), that
ridiculous shred of fabric twisted about her neck only ag-
gravates the uncharacteristic inelegance of my girlfriend's
outfit, a worn pink shirt with gray stripes, a suit, bulging at
the seams, blue: it's Louis-René Raffin, her father, frozen in
place, staring at us.

"But how do you keep from falling?"

That's all he can find to say, his one and only question. He's probing the trade secrets of the housefly when what he should be wondering is why beings no different from himself would choose to make their home on the ceiling. But no matter how little he cares about our motivations, I confess that I would be curious to know his, I would gladly hear him enumerate the many excellent features that keep him glued to the floor. It's true: from here, because of his girth and because our vertical viewpoint flattens both volume and perspective, Louis-René Raffin appears to be fused to the floor as a duck to water: you can't see his webbed feet. He almost looks as though he's taken root, or is slowly sinking in, boring a hole with his belly. Unless he's melting, Malton's got a point, he does seem to be melting, or rather collapsing in upon himself, his narrow skull and sloping shoulders form the peak of a mountain eaten away from below, slowly crumbling at the edges and spreading in all directions, in the end it will become a puddle or a lawn. Méline could not possibly have been born of his seed, with every fiber of my being I resist the idea of such a repugnant incestuous act as the engendering of daughters by their own fathers – no, the great cresting wave atop which the little girl's cradle floated must merely have rolled over onto a naked shoulder, depositing the child into the arms of the woman gasping for air below.

Who, having put her clothes on again, having combed her hair again, having aged twenty years, joins him in the hallway:

"How do you keep from falling?"

In some couples, husband and wife are not so much complementary as redundant. Clotilde Raffin dresses in animal pelts; even in her apartment she wears plush stoles and stuffed slippers – nowadays, after having long patronized animal farmers and trappers, moved like so many others by the cruel fate awaiting the marmot, the sable, and the blue fox, she wears only synthetic furs, coats, muffs, toques, cuffed booties, and so, in order to feed the lucrative market for substitutes, victims of a terrible, silent carnage, entire populations of virtual animals are decimated every year, without a word of protest from anyone, their dismembered corpses rotting in our dreams, polluting our imaginations.

Alert and aquiver at his mistress's heels, Woff, neither mink nor seal, frizzy and black, not a karakul lamb either, seems to be greatly excited by our presence, and he runs zigzags through the hallway, he leaps up clumsily in a vain attempt at achieving liftoff so that he can come and join us. He can't understand why his paws won't do his bidding, he sprints forward, he stands up against the walls, he even forces his ears into a double helicoidal motion that, although the most ludicrous and least effective of his efforts, is probably also the only one with any real chance of success; if, that is, this is indeed an example of the sort of corrective gymnastics that instinct devises so as to better adapt the individual to his surroundings, then Woff's distant descendants, mutants equipped with a double-bladed propeller for vertical takeoff, will one day rise up and join us.

"But how do you keep from falling?"

So say Monsieur and Madame, with one voice, dully insistent.

To pose such a question is to trivialize our project and our ambitions. For it should be obvious that we did not come up to the ceiling to go on living the life of those below – we will not play stalactite to their stalagmite. With a little altitude, many things that once seemed enormously significant begin to take on more modest proportions, and the loftier your perch, the more numerous the whales in the deep fryer, my favorite meal, cooked in their own oil, and, in the same way, human concerns come to seem pettier and paltrier, so much so that God's apathy toward their affairs might well constitute the very proof of His existence, at the highest summit of the heavens.

The ceiling is the ideal surface for the exercise of the human mind, which in any other spot must focus on the development of offensive or defensive strategies for coping with the conditions at hand. From the earliest times, man's beleaguered genius has exhausted itself coming up with solutions to his problems. He invents the ice ax at the foot of the mountain and then, having reached the summit, he invents skis to get back down again, all very clever, always after the path of least resistance, but what if the mountain hadn't been there? The bridge is an elegant creation of his mind, a solid work of art wrought by the strength of his arm: man's way of digging in his heels against the power of the river. And what if that river hadn't been there? As a refuge from nature's hostility we have built the city, an orderly gridwork space, under our control, in which every problem encountered outside its walls finds a solution, for in the final analysis the city is nothing other than the systematization of all our solutions to all the problems that have ever threatened our survival, without which the city would have no reason to exist. And it displays the failings, the flaws, the missteps to be found in any solution, by definition secondary to and determined by its problem, whose blunt immediacy is never weakened by ambiguities of this sort. The anxiety remains, the city, permanently on edge, seems always about to explode, the inhabitants live in fear, they throw up additional defenses, private ones, inside the walls of this armed camp, and in this unsettled, tiptoe existence, they suffer even more agonizingly than if they had struggled on in the grips of their original torments. But those torments are the very font of our existence, because it is only in relation to them that we can take up a position and fight back, or at least learn to resign ourselves, and also because man has never had a chance to pursue his ideas in some neutral, virgin space, open to the unconstrained application of his gifts. The ceiling is that space, even if by projection it duplicates the shape of the rooms it overhangs, in this case the Raffins' apartment, meaning that we have no choice but to make do with that structure. That alone lies beyond our control, at least in part, for it would not be out of the question to undertake a few small renovations. No matter. The Earth outside is round, and there's no way around that either.

"We'll see," says Topouria.

*

In the beginning, the heavens were unencumbered by living things, the world ended in a point atop the highest mountain, itself uninhabited. The plain was the place for animals, crawling or otherwise, their bellies scraped the ground, their tails dragged through the mud. Here and there, you can still spot one of those old trails and follow it. But suddenly it breaks off: the bird flew away, without waiting for feathers, no time for that, it took wing, it threw itself into the void, the situation on the ground was becoming untenable. But then the birds declared war among themselves. Their flight path curved in on itself, sank earthward, they dove to catch fish beneath the surface of the water or worms living underground. Soon it was clear that their miraculous flight was mere pie in the sky – their white eggs among the branches are the bulging eyes of hanged men with a bad case of vertigo.

Whether Madame Stempf is talking about birds or something else, we drink in her words, we still have much to learn from her, are we not her newborn children? This world above the world is the very one she had dreamt of for us. Here we have everything we need, the atmospheric pressure keeps germs and viruses at bay, we have nothing to fear but our own reflexes, unsuited to these new circumstances, and we must work to reform them if we hope to succeed on the ceiling in an enterprise at which the birds have already failed in the sky.

Kolski, Topouria, the bunch, we didn't live by the rules down below, no argument there, but up here there's nothing strange about our behavior, nothing aberrant. For the first time, we sense that our characters do not clash with our surroundings, but, on the contrary, merge with them and move through them with perfect ease. But that's precisely where the danger lies. In our element, relaxed, at peace, we might be tempted to think ourselves no different from those below, and to do as they do – a simian reflex that we must cast off, for it would bring about our downfall. Elevation, for instance, is a meaningless concept on the ceiling, where nothing protrudes or looms; but foolishly I saw myself as an orator at his podium, or a lecturer on his rostrum, or a preacher in his pulpit, or a general on his hilltop, or a prophet on his mount, as if I were looking up at myself from the ground, or from the valley, from the bottom of the ditch, tilting my head back, and I made a speech, a sort of homily at least, or a lesson, on the mercilessness of nature and the ruthlessness of the city, that sort of thing, nothing very original. Worse yet, when laid end to end those considerations form a sketchy but compelling argument that might be seen as an attempt to justify our coming to the ceiling. But I have no interest in pleading our case. I don't mind being thought a madman, and I long ago gave up hoping I might persuade others to follow my lead, back in the days of my first humiliations, when I blazed a trail through the crowd with my chair on my head, garnering jibes and sneers rather than the immediate universal following I was expecting, and which I thought I had a right to expect, having forgotten that the obvious truth is the one no one can see, and overestimating the pedagogical efficacy of example – they wouldn't have shunned me more vigorously if I'd been wearing mittens on my feet, a clock on my shoulder, something ridiculous like that.

Nevertheless, I must admit that I would like to lure Méline to the ceiling. Our fingers brush halfway up, occasionally interlace, she's as light as the water you draw from a well to quench your thirst, I could easily lift her up – and then what? start a family? closet myself away with her in the double egotism, more hermetically closed than any circle, of an amorous relationship? Two lovers locked in mutual contemplation, each lost in the other's gaze, need only exchange eyes once and for all in order to find their way out of that blind alley, then, cramming them into their new orbits with their thumbs, turn that double stare back onto the world, enthralling it in turn, so as to remake it in accordance with the infallible laws of love, which could then spread unhindered until it covered the entire surface of the globe – and then what? start a church? the honey that flows from gargoyles makes the stickiest tarpits, I'd be happier in the mud, smiles float on it at least, and sail onward. On the ceiling, we will have to take great care not to fall back into the mistaken ways of the world below.

*

Where Méline is struggling without success to calm her parents, who, losing patience, order Hans to get himself back down to the floor, and step on it *(sic)*. Hotly, he refuses, only his blood descends, his father's blood, more obedient than he, begins to make its way toward the floor, reddens his face. You're going to die of apoplexy if you keep it up, screams Raffin, very angry, very red himself, apparently forgetting that blood also rises whenever people get hot under the collar, the mercury of the mercurial temperament, and Madame, terrified, awaits the moment when both father's and son's heads will explode under the pressure, the last few liters of Raffin blood bursting out like lightning bolts, then falling like rain onto the carpet, bringing about the extinction, for lack of male heirs, of the proud lineage that has given our land so many great men, devoted servants, merry cobblers, old geezers, misunderstood geniuses, innocent bystanders, crafty peasants, valiant soldiers, mischievous tykes, proper authorities, luscious lasses, lone gunmen, tiny dwarves, inveterate drunkards, unlicensed lawyers, enraptured lovers, jolly fatsoes, hardy seamen, alert shopkeepers, confirmed tomboys, happy husbands, chronic invalids, down through the centuries, and what a shame that would be, I have to do something, without delay, delegate the task of soothing tempers to one of my companions, Lanson, of whom I've asked almost nothing, a rather underused character, long relegated to the chore of pushing Malton's wheelchair, of which he acquitted himself in his own way, as carefree as if he were going for a spin in a horse-drawn carriage, with Malton playing the role of the horse, but now he has found a place where his talents can come into full bloom, Lanson, make yourself useful for once in your life, we're waiting to hear what you have to say.

"The sloth is an edentate mammal endowed with the same number of little gray teeth as Geoffroy Saint-Hilaire, common throughout the forests of South America, remarkable for the slow agility with which it moves among the trees and for its long periods of motionlessness, turning its back to the ground, using the three curved claws of its four limbs like hooks in order to hang from the branches, moving nothing but its head, a remarkably mobile head, able to rotate through 270 degrees, thanks to its nine cervical vertebrae, allowing easy access to the fruits, leaves, and flowers on which the animal feeds, which often grow back as its head continues its rotation so that the sloth needn't think of leaving his branch for quite some time, and butterflies lay their eggs in its fur, home to cyanophyta sprouts as well, and those greenish microscopic algae lend its matted pelt the look of some vegetal phenomenon, sufficiently convincing to fool the jaguars, no great fans of salad as we know, and it's their loss, for this one would be tender and juicy, just the way they like it, with bones. The sloth makes no provisions for its own safety, it is the most untroubled animal in the whole of Creation. Without even working at it, through sheer inertia, it has crafted a body truly built for sloth: its fur parts along the center line of its breast and belly rather than its spine and falls over its ribs in such a way as to speed the shedding of rainwater; better yet, its organs have gradually shifted according to their weight and mass, the liver no longer weighs on the stomach; the spleen, entrails, and pancreas have slipped away from their original locations with no loss of efficiency, quite the reverse, for the sloth defecates only once a week, approximately – approximately! – showing wonderful self-control, and its lazy cardiac and respiratory rates guarantee it an astonishing longevity for an animal weighing no more than nine kilograms, a lifespan far longer than terrestrial mammals of related species could ever hope for or fear, falling victim as they inevitably do to predators or accidents, and whose vital energy is consumed at a higher rate, as you see, you have nothing to fear. Hans will soon adapt to the ideal conditions he has found here, he will only be the better for it, already he has escaped the range of your slaps and smacks – the heavier the hand of the father, the fleeter the foot of the son, it's a law of heredity – but, if you are still not convinced that his place is here among us, I would be happy to speak to you now of the marvelous life of the bat?"

*

Louis-René Raffin takes a step back, defeated, his strength deserting him as if he had been drained of his substance as he vented his anger, he sags nearer the ground than ever, this time he really does seem to be about to sink into the floor or go down to the cellar, he slumps, staggers like a drunkard, giddy, perhaps, from having kept his eyes raised toward the ceiling for so long, there's a price to be paid for breathing the rarefied air of the mountaintop, you need an elevated soul, unless you have specially trained lungs, his wife and his daughter support him as they retreat toward the door. He turns around one last time before crossing the threshold.

"Tell us at least how you keep from falling?"

But his question, too, is left hanging.

It's hard to free ourselves completely. Life on the ceiling
would be better if we didn't have to hear the sounds of life
below as clearly as if we squatted there still. The Raffin
couple's conversation is not the kind that examines questions of piezoelectricity or Orphic themes in painting,
even if Louis-René likes to address his wife as though he
were standing before an audience of a hundred thousand,
unintimidated by the size of the crowd, speaking in a voice
that never quavers, braving the catcalls that his bold policy
statement might provoke, he offers her his recommen-
dations for, in his words, pulling our civilization out of
this stagnant slough, one might find similar words in the
mouths of swamp-dwelling carps, who would die of thirst
in more limpid waters. Ordinarily, thanks to the interplay
of associated ideas, the freewheeling logic of conversation
will lead two participants in a tête-à-tête far from their
original subject, soon they're exchanging confidences,
pleasantries, the occasional prophecy is fulfilled the moment it is uttered – the rheumatism, heralding the coming
of a storm, bolts from the old prophet's knee and shoots
between the clouds – they venture odd ideas or divergent
opinions, they progress, in short, without method or
goal, they advance, hypotheses at least, anecdotes, bizarre
or scabrous, are judiciously inserted to illustrate their
thoughts: you know Father Clément, so stern and unbend-
ing when it comes to morality, so unsympathetic in his

treatment of fallen women, who gives us a sermon every Sunday and boasts incessantly of the chaste and frugal life he leads, well can you imagine, it was him, one summer day back in 1902, who hitched up his cassock, spread the modestly clenched thighs of a Mandarin with his long cruciform hands, and conceived that little Clementine. But the Raffins' conversation, apart from politics, revolves around household affairs and nothing else, the same domestic axioms are repeated day after day, the same answers to the same queries, sometimes, however, with tiny variants that serve to test the system's stability, its capacity to assimilate some new element, some unexpected fact, without collapsing or derailing: thanks to these daily exercises, a family crisis could suddenly rear its head, a death for instance, without serious harm to its functioning – has Hans not already gone to Heaven in a sense, and, now that the initial shock has passed, has life below not resumed its usual course? Furthermore, we must recognize that our presence on the ceiling has already ceased to disturb the Raffins, whereas we, ourselves, are tortured by our overcrowded conditions, unendingly, by the noise from below, the comings and goings. The monotonous spectacle put before us takes up far more of our attention than I would like, it's keeping us from the task of making a permanent home here. We're still only camping out. We still share light and darkness, cold, heat, with those below, and we're not in a position to command those forces. The Raffins determine the length of day and night, we are continually exposed to their music and their cooking, so intimately related in their inspiration that the swells of the one and the scents of the other come together, the ear and the nose enter into collaboration, suddenly the air grows thicker, as if choked with flies, we have to hack our way through it with our elbows, for that sludge clings to our bodies as well: the ambiance is upon us.

*

I've spent too many years on the floor, my nauseated senses long for open space, my thin-skinned blood juggles with daggers, never will worms slither through my corpse in such great numbers as the nerves that eat me alive. In the daytime, once Raffins Louis-René and Clotilde have left, I can finally rest: on the ceiling, the eye makes a bed in the great expanse of white, the vertical body stretches out with a sigh, blissfully comfortable, for silence is the only pillow worthy of the name. Allergic to feathers like the rest of us, birds are tossed into the air by their sneezes, Madame Stempf informs me, I'm not surprised to hear it, the only reason they beat their wings is to further irritate their sensitive mucus membranes – a bird immune will soon make its nest among fried potatoes or hot chestnuts, it doesn't stand a chance of escaping the old peasant woman already on its tail, who loses a house-slipper as she runs,

slips it back on again, stops to pick a few herbs for season-
ing, catches the bird, and wrings its neck.

Then the Raffins return, the racket resumes, they have no
inhibitions before us, to say the least. In the living room,
Louis-René unfolds his newspaper and reads to Clotilde,
hard at work in the kitchen, just as if they were all alone –
when on one occasion a match skillfully tossed by Malton
set the paper ablaze, he didn't even seem to notice and went
on coolly turning the pages, apprising his wife (who was
busy cutting up the poultry she'd bought at the market
from an old peasant woman in slippers who tossed in a *bou-
quet garni* for free) of the astonishing tale of a pyromaniac,
the day's top story, who, after having set fire to the Houses
of Parliament, the Stock Exchange, the powder keg of the
Balkans, the four corners of the globe, returned to his home
town, burned down the theater, the movie houses, the horse
track, the stadium, and last of all the courthouse, where he
allowed himself to become surrounded by the flames, look,
darling, at all these ashes on the rug.

And when Topouria, rerouting a water pipe, sent a powerful gush spraying over Clotilde and her talkative friends
from the prayer and meditation group, of which she serves
as treasurer, meeting that night to debate the proper stance
to adopt when our children lose their faith – should we nag
them, loudly bemoan their blindness, argue, show them the
flaws in their reasoning and evoke all the great minds who

could not have been wrong in such large numbers, or allude darkly to the threat of divine punishment, yes, but if we take that route do we not run the risk of further hardening their hearts, of giving them an excuse to break with religion forever, or should we allow them to express their opinion, pretend to consider it so seriously that it shakes us in our own faith, then triumph over our doubts before their very eyes in the hope that they will follow our lead, or perhaps, placing our faith in their spirit of contradiction, trust that they will find their faith again if we claim to have lost ours, yes, but if we take that route, deceitfully putting on an act that carries, moreover, no guarantee of success, are we not violating the teachings of our Lord, or should we, finally, hold our peace and respect their choice without attempting to hide our sorrow, pray for their enlightenment, and humbly offer them the example of our good Christian life, a life of generosity and compassion, yes, but if we take that route, will we not become in their eyes nothing more than good people, worthy of their esteem and dear to their hearts, oh it's not an easy problem – that cold shower had a certain effect on them, but they attributed it to their conversation, to the despondent realization of their own impotence and the shattering of their last remaining illusions.

*

But we are not entirely helpless should the need arise for

action or reprisal. The Raffins may fear neither water nor fire, but we can at least deprive them of light by unscrewing the bulbs in all the ceilings throughout the apartment, breaking that egg which fries its chick in an attempt to scintillate, and it would be no less feasible for us to close the curtains whenever they open them, or the reverse, rolling the Moon into their rooms in the middle of the night. But the fact is that we didn't come up here just to go on waging war against those below, despite the new weapons at our disposal and the incontestable advantage our air power gives us (everything we drop hits a target and causes damage). On the floor, we lived through one painful setback after another, from morning to night, we played the part of the humiliated victim, now the situation has turned to our favor, vertically we tower over the others, we won't take advantage of it. We have better things to do. But would it not be possible to arrive at something like a non-aggression pact, of the kind one often finds among the better sort of neighbors, by establishing a border halfway up, for example? I don't mean stretching barbed wire from wall to wall, of course, a theoretical border would be sufficient, but an inviolable one, with any incursion rendering the treaty null and void. Maximum permissible noise levels would be strictly regulated on either side, and a common schedule would be worked out, by mutual agreement, for the rising and setting of the sun, nothing more than that, and above all no commercial trade, we've paid our dues.

✶

To the mind of a man such as Louis-René Raffin, however, the peopling of the ceilings can only mean the opening of a new market, and a juicy new market, too, he believes, assuming that we lack even the most basic necessities. I imagine he's working out a plan to take advantage of his good fortune, since, as it happened, the conquest of the ceilings began in his home, he's probably hoping to secure exclusive rights to our patronage, and beat out the competition in the race to sign the first contracts. Let's not forget that the man works for a major import-export company, where his widely recognized talents as an importer are alas not counterbalanced by equal talents as an exporter, meaning that the sector over which he presides posts a serious deficit at the end of every month, and he, himself, suffers a similar discredit in the eyes of the board of directors. Here, he thinks, is the chance to redress the balance and restore his image at the same time. He spares no effort. With Clotilde's assistance, pretending not to realize we're there, he launches into laborious product demonstrations beneath our gaze, in hopes of selling us all the things we lack on the ceiling, of equipping us fully, from the most basic necessities to the most modern household appliances (two out of three primatologists agree: the recent invention of the electric banana-peeler is an event second in importance only to the adoption of the erect posture eight million years ago).

The sales pitch begins the moment he returns from the office: no sooner has he crossed the threshold of the apartment than he hangs his overcoat on the rack planted in the front hallway like a tree, wild cherry, which never bends, not even when squalls of wind and snow force Clotilde to take her heaviest furs from the closet, then Louis-René kicks off his shoes, and, smiling vapidly, slips into buttery-soft black leather slippers, brand-new, and his wife, smiling vapidly, casually asks if he wouldn't prefer the brown ones or the burgundy ones, he answers no, he did hesitate for a moment over the yellow ones, and the blue ones aren't bad either, and so we learn that these slippers come in five colors, but by now the Raffins are in the living room, praising the plush luxuriousness of the hand-knotted rug (all the agility of the hand in the service of the foot, that bumbling, ungainly extremity), ornamented with shapes of Persian origin, 300 x 400 cm, congratulating themselves on not having chosen one of the smaller sizes, 170 x 240 cm or 200 x 300 cm, then sinking into a deep but convex sofa that lets out a double sigh of contentment as it receives them, sparing them that trouble as well, and they stroke its cushions with the palms of their hands as if the young cow were still lucid enough to appreciate their caresses.

"What a dreary little room you've got there," exclaims Kolski, "and what an ugly bench, are you waiting for an appointment with the dentipsychoanalyst so he can help you spit out your baby teeth? Allow me to suggest a few small improvements: to begin with, don't cut the tails off the bovines you flay to make coverings for your armchairs and your sofa, that way they can go on swinging that tireless fly swatter, with which the living animal is equipped for a reason, as you'll see when springtime comes, when the horseflies attack, or in October, when the dying flies fall onto your face like rain, great warm disgusting drops that you won't be able to brush away, the swarm will devour you alive, and you'll eat some of them as well – how utterly repulsive, even the spiders won't touch them when they're that overripe."

The Raffins turn a deaf ear and continue their spiel, everything gets a mention, everything is for sale, the glass from which Louis-René drinks, the whisky itself, aged twelve years, and the ice cube that makes it seem ten years younger, the table set for dinner, the dishes, the silverware, the chairs too . . . they clearly don't understand us, their furniture is precisely the sort of relic we want nothing more to do with, and what they call bare necessities, we call junk, utterly useless to us on the ceiling.

＊

As for the rich cultural exchanges that have become customary between neighboring continents, we solemnly launch the program by returning to the Raffins all the various works of art that now sully our wainscoting. From our half of the walls, Kolski unhooks ten or twelve photographic reproductions of paintings so well known that they no longer have a top or bottom, and so remain unaltered no matter what angle they might be viewed from – indelibly imprinted on our retinas, they have taken on the curve of our eyeball and become spherical, evoked in their entirety by their smallest detail, as if each of the colored dots making up such a picture did indeed contain it, identical to itself, miniaturized and multiplied within the frame until the entire canvas is covered. At the same time, having been left exposed to daylight without protection, these reproductions have faded, for the fact is that light hates to leave a trail behind it, and works tirelessly to erase every last trace of its passage; given time, it would replace them all with the same pale rectangles that Kolski reveals as he takes them down from the wall: he is only anticipating or hastening the action of the light, which despite its prodigious rate of propagation is still too long in coming for this impatient soul, and so he runs on ahead of it. Beneath the reproductions, the walls are as white as the day they were made, they haven't aged. They've never been used. They've shirked the common task of supporting the building's floors and frame. Indignant, Kolski plans to paint a fresco over every inch of the surface of the walls except these trompe l'oeils, which will henceforth have to bear the entire burden of the building by themselves – same punishment for the plaster virgin in the living room, so cozy and comfortable in her little arched niche, she'll be crushed, pulverized, if she doesn't make like a caryatid and make it snappy.

Also displayed on our walls are examples of the Raffins' more personal artistic tastes: that cornered deer is done for unless it can find a way across the chasm, several centimeters wide, separating it from the next painting over, where a peaceful herd is grazing in a pool of green paint; the deer could easily conceal itself in their midst, given its own strong resemblance to a bull; elsewhere on the wall, a sick seascape, and, crafted by the same hand, or the other one, a traditional composition depicting a bowl of poisoned fruit, a bottle full of glass, a knife thrust deep between the ribs of a loaf of bread or bayonetted infant, a painting particularly notable for its use of chiaroscuro, as subtly distributed as on a chessboard. In the front hallway, a cork panel is studded with photographs of the Raffin family, for each of which, thanks to Louis-René's concentric bellies, we could easily determine a precise date, and so establish a chronology, but for the moment they are tacked up in no particular order: here he is, for instance, with a prize fishing catch, whose heft the visitor is invited to gauge with his eyes, careful, if you close one eye you'll drop it; you then stare uncertainly at the portrait in gray and yellow, lace-edged, dog-eared, of an ethereal, bare-shouldered goddess (pretend to recognize Clotilde without the slightest difficulty); the children are there as well, in a stroller, on bicycles, at the beach, in the garden, and, finally, on an outdoor stage, Hans, fitted with a red nose and false bald head, poses next to a nymph oddly disguised as a little girl smeared with chocolate.

Malton takes down the canvases and the cork panel, with Egger's enthusiastic help he goes on to cast into the void everything encroaching on our half of the walls, the books sitting on the topmost shelves, the piles of linen and sheets from the upper reaches of the closets. In his bedroom, Hans himself tears down the full-length portraits of his screeching idols, frozen mute by the photographer but still grimacing, hunched over their guitars, and, so, still expressive enough to disturb the sleep of the neighbors on the other side of the wall.

These crumpled posters, these paintings, these books, these clothes strewn randomly about the floor, without a word Méline picks it all up and puts it all away, restores order, I call out to her, I extend my hand, she will grasp it, and I'll carry her away from her family, gently lift her from the floor and set her down beside me on the ceiling, her skirt, flying up, will uncover her loins, I'll lead her into the living room, we'll lie beneath the ceiling light, a silver-leaved aspen, and our son, born into this free land, will be the first man fully fit to live here, light of heart, clear of head, a boy with a future. Méline smiles, takes my hand, clasps my arm, hangs on tight – she's a flower waiting to be picked – suddenly gives it a twist, turning on her toes like a ballerina, and, with a strength I would never have suspected, pulls me downward and tries to throw me to the floor, I resist, with a jerk of my body I break free. Méline weeps, one large tear, single and mute, the exhaustive tear of very small children, the eye rolling onto the cheek – then the bedroom's plush carpeting absorbs it.

Let me clear up a misunderstanding that might have arisen from my various observations and commentaries concerning the Raffins' life on the floor, as if by concentrating on their acts and deeds, as I have done for the past few weeks, I were putting off the work that must be undertaken if we are to settle here and make a life for ourselves on the ceiling. You might have thought I'd suddenly lost my nerve when I glimpsed the immense range of possibilities lying open to our ambition, or that I was terrified by the vast scale of the task before us, or that I didn't know how or where to begin. Or that, prone to vertigo, as I hang here above the void, gripped by panic, I was clinging to the floor with my eyes, my gaze fixed in desperate longing on the world we left behind, concealing my spite or homesickness behind a rather facile sort of mockery, concealing also my grief at having failed to find a place for myself down below. Or else that my hopes had gone unfulfilled on the ceiling, that the gossamer wings of my dreams had been cruelly broken here and that I couldn't bear to admit it, not even to myself. But no, I have not lost my faith, make no mistake. I do not dwell on the Raffins in order to accentuate our differences from them and so to define ourselves in relation to them, surely the hawk is not a mere satellite of the hare. No: in our disgust with life on the floor, and in our weariness of that very disgust, we found the impetus we needed to reach the ceiling – and having scaled the heights, I simply wanted to prove to myself that our reasons were sound. As for vertigo, given that I have for so long managed to resist my attraction to Méline, to her smile and her tears, to the supplications of her frustrated affection, to the ample forms of her slender body, generous to me and to no one else, it should be clear that I am hardly likely to give in now to the lure of the void.

*

Building, sowing, planting, such things never enter our mind, no more than exploiting the natural resources we would find if we scratched at or dug into the surface beneath our feet, chiefly gypsum: rather, our thoughts are of enlarging our territory. As with the desert or the sea, there's no point in trying to erect walls on the ceiling, it will always be the same on either side. Walls might seem a good idea on the floor, where division rules the day, where each room, set aside for a particular purpose, is consequently (or, more precisely, in preparation for the consequences of its purpose) tiled, parqueted, lined with carpet or linoleum, but the concept is perfectly meaningless on the ceiling, where we stand far above such small concerns – when the ceiling's surface flakes and blackens in the kitchen or the bathroom, it is because of the same phenomenon of condensation that creates clouds in the sky, you can hardly call that a simple domestic event.

The friezes and rosettes that decorate the ceilings of

some sitting rooms are, for the most part, nothing more than add-ons, made of wood or stucco or molded plaster, applied at some later date to that plain, smooth background, white and indestructible; the more rarely seen coffers, painted or gilded, hanging from the ceiling like little caskets awaiting dead souls, can be just as easily removed (what would we ever keep in those boxes, our stockpiles of what, our letters from whom, what souvenirs, what files, what tools?). Only exposed beams will have to be left in place, except for the false ones, properly varnished and protruding but hollow, like the muscles of some pneumatic, oiled colossus lifting weights on Atlas's back, and those we will crush beneath our heels: they feign enormous effort, even going so far as to bow slightly beneath the weight of their imaginary burden and trying to pass off as their own the groans of the building's actual frame, locked away in the attic, whose horrific load they make even heavier, if only by a little – for, in truth, that pitiful clutch of matchsticks weighs next to nothing. But the ceilings with exposed, honest beams, beams made of wood full of wood, solid, those will be our horizontal forests, stripped of their branches, impervious to the changing seasons, which have all come and gone so many times now that they seem simultaneous, and, hence, time itself nearly immobile, and so at long last time will be returned to us, dynamic, fluid, as open as the horizon whose view our forest of beams will never block, a usable time, unhindered, even capable of an occasional acceleration, the impossibility of which is a particularly irritating absurdity where seasons are concerned: for autumn's filthy task, fifteen minutes well spent ought to be enough.

Calculate the combined surface area of all the available ceilings in the world and you will find the area of the terrain open to us for expansion – it's enormous. By available ceilings, I mean those currently unoccupied, on the one hand, and practicable, on the other, so excluding the arched vaults found in churches, too steep, or in igloos, too slippery, the ceiling-roofs that cover all sorts of precarious dwellings made of canvas, branches, wattle and daub, too fragile, and the summits of certain gymnasia, occasionally frequented by trapeze artists. But these fairly significant restrictions should not be taken to mean that the inhabitable surface of the floor exceeds what we have before us on the ceiling. We must remember that our space is unencumbered by furniture (a grand piano in a house means a quartet out on the street), we own no beds, no tables, no televisions, no washing machines, no bathtubs. There are impenetrable cupboards and storage spaces to which we alone will have access. And we can live more comfortably in ruins than the others: if the ceiling of a building has collapsed, it will be of no good to us, but even if the floor was sound, those who live below wouldn't want to run the risk of having a roof-beam fall on their heads, and they have a similar fear of rain and snow, so they wouldn't want to live there either; on the other hand, if the floor of a building has collapsed, it will be of no good to them, but so long as the ceiling is sound, we can still make our home there, protected against all inclemencies.

In a general sense, life is less risky on the ceiling. We fear neither floods – it's unlikely that faulty plumbing or a river dragged from its bed by a cloudburst would ever spew four meters of water into a house, and, even if it did, we'd be the last ones drowned – or animal infestations – whereas on the floor, ants form vast caravans, some red, some black, and feed their larvae on the luscious grain left out to poison the mice, which prefer to dine on the lemon peels intended to drive away the ants. Clotilde did, however, once threaten us with the angrily bristling head of a broom when Topouria, armed with a short length of lead pipe, set out to demolish the wall separating Hans's room from Méline's, the upper half of the wall at least, our half, for the time of the expansion has come, but our first thought as we felt its whiskers nuzzling at our legs and heard the accompanying snarl was that Woff had finally made the leap and come to join us, although Woff is certainly no wolf – besides, there's no such thing as wolves, interjects Madame Stempf, their footprints in the snow are only inkblots on the storyteller's page, and he's too lazy to copy it out again neatly, he'd rather tell hurtful lies about mysterious prowlers, completely fabricated, even today he blames them whenever he devours a little girl. But no, it was only a broom that Clotilde, equally disheveled on the other end of the handle, had raised against us when she should have been tending to her own house, down below: I've never seen a place so badly kept up, there's dust all over the floor and all over the furniture, there are even piles of rubble lying here and there.

The thinner interior walls, made of brick and plaster, those you can poke holes in with your fist, they shatter with a single touch, they disintegrate like meringue into little chunks, into a fine powder, almost smoke, first white, then tinged with orange, which sticks to our skin, we look like Indians, the vast plain stretching out before us, unfenced, as its barriers come down. Having demolished the wall between the bedrooms, Topouria next turns to the one that runs the length of the hallway and defines its limits. His aim is true, expressed through violent blows both regular and precise, the division halfway up the wall is clean and straight, even the doors are still aligned, sliced in two: thus vertically reduced by half, the Raffins' apartment recalls the compartmentalized drawers in tool boxes or portable medicine chests, or better yet one of those toy ranches in whose open-air enclosures crouching children stage confrontations between plastic figurines of cows and cowboys; and, in fact, I do believe that we could easily grasp Clotilde or Louis-René between thumb and index finger and play with them, as if they had shrunk or we had monstrously grown – instead we chose to rise even further above them, this time for real, by bashing down what's left of the walls connecting the ceiling to the floor. We have truly burned our bridges. We have taken to the skies.

I like to think we're not alone, I like to believe that here and there other teams are working as we are to bring down the walls, so that we might someday consolidate our fragmented holdings and unite all our little isolated groups, some of which might be struggling merely to survive, for conditions are undoubtedly not as favorable everywhere as at the Raffins'. Arrogant and ungenerous, the majority of property owners believe that they also own the air contained within their dwellings, and the walls as well, from top to bottom, and the ceilings, where they nonetheless never set foot, on which they are all the more reluctant to loosen their grip because they themselves do not have the power to grasp them. And they will not stop at brandishing brooms – rifles come out of their cases, pitchforks are sharpened, ladders are leaned against the walls – we have a duty to come to the aid of our scattered peers, to offer them temporary shelter while we await the opportunity to return in force and retake the ceilings. One day the numbers will be with us. Young civilizations are always the most vital, a fresher, richer blood irrigates their children's flesh, and the bones that hold up their bodies have never rested in a graveyard's ashy soil.

*

We still run into walls. The apartment's four exterior walls, thicker and more solid than the others, do not give way when smashed with a club. Topouria can't make a dent in the one he's currently assailing. Beside him, Egger manages to break off a few little shards, fine and translucent, working with his bare hands, breaking his fingernails. We're left, then, with a surface of some 160 square meters, equal to that of the Raffins' apartment but more spacious because undivided and unfurnished, with plenty of elbow room. If we want to go beyond that, we have only two exits to choose from: the windows or the door that opens onto the landing. We could undoubtedly break through the ceiling itself, but then we would be back on the floor, in the apartment above, and that we cannot accept. On the other hand, we could easily make our way into the adjoining apartments – every floor has four of them identical to this one – and break down the doors. Once inside, we could demolish the interior walls, as we have here, then use the elevator to progress to the floors above and below us, a dozen in all, and so enlarge our territory by that much (without once touching the ground) – we would nonetheless remain prisoners of the building itself. We'll go through the windows, then. They all overlook the street, except the one in the kitchen, which, giving as good as it gets, gives onto a courtyard and gets a bit of light in return, albeit a very meager bit, despite the magnifying effect of the circles of bottle glass in the window's stationary upper half, like the thick lenses of the resident myopic, who has been known to go wrong sorting pumpkins from cherries and has often come close to plunging Woff into boiling water, but the drooling little beast that lives with the Raffins is no crab.

We stand at the windows, Lanson and Malton over the kitchen, the others over the living room and the bedrooms (these reductive toponyms have lost all meaning for us), and survey the facing buildings, paying particular attention to the apartments on the same level as ours. For we will need allies if we are to cross the street, allies who will help us build a footbridge from one side to the other. Such superstructures, running from building to building, modernized, reinforced so as to prevent swaying in high winds – we're not acrobats! – will be a common sight in the future. The technical difficulties of the project are of little importance. Our ingenuity is always ready for a challenge. For now, we only need to meet up with a gaze from across the way, the forming of that first link above the void will allow us to dream the wildest dreams. But the connection will have to be stable enough to carry us to the other side just as we are, it being understood that we will step onto it without concession or compromise, head held high toward the ground, as at present.

*

What if the sign of recognition we are searching for never comes? Once it has insinuated itself into his mind, that doubt robs the searcher of his vigilance, and so becomes a reality in its own unforeseeable way – after three days on the trail without a sighting, the tiger-hunter loses faith in the whole undertaking, you can snarl in his ear, lick his eye, lacerate his stomach with your claws, and eat his liver; he sadly packs up his rifle and leaves the area, disappointed, everyone said this was such a great place to hunt. Our forced immobility preys on our minds. Beneath us, the Raffins have swept up the debris and dusted off the furniture. They keep up their daily occupations, timed down to the minute, their amusements are the habits they cling to the most grimly. They're no longer disturbed by our presence. Even now, Louis-René sometimes lifts his head and looks at us wearily – how do you keep from falling? – the question springs mechanically to his lips, but he doesn't insist, he doesn't seem to care whether he gets an answer or not. He seems far more curious about the outcome of the day's cliffhanger, the name of the winner of a district election or of a grand prix car race that has spent the afternoon going round in circles, and did the hunting party that set off into the forest this morning finally put an end to the mysterious Beast that has been decimating the herds, wild dog, degenerate bear, fleeing puma, or what, and did the surgeons decide to go ahead and amputate the second cerebral hemisphere of the old leader of the young country lying in ruins down the road? Ready for anything, Louis-René Raffin settles in before his television set. This would not be the time to break our silence and answer his question. Still, it's an interesting question, I have to recognize that. When you think about it, it's even a rather troublesome question, says Kolski, if you accept the idea that every mass is subject to a centripetal force directed toward the center of the Earth, on the one hand, and a centrifugal force arising from the rotation of the Earth, on the other, and that the result of these two forces is gravity, which no one can resist.